From the mome ... **the ranch, Theo had known an attack was possible. Likely, even.**

But it still gave him an adrenaline spike to see that weapon now pointed at Gabriel's house.

Ivy's breathing was already way too fast, and Theo considered trying to do something to help her level it. But if he pulled her into his arms now, it would definitely be a distraction, and he needed to keep his attention on the rifle.

It was already dark, but there was enough of a moon to see the light glint off the barrel. Enough to see, too, when the barrel shifted just a little, and Theo spotted the scope on it.

"A shot from there would be able to make it here," she said.

It wasn't a question. She knew it could. But he hated to hear the slight tremble in her voice.

Theo watched as the barrel shifted again, and he steeled himself for what he figured would come next. He didn't have to wait long.

The gunman fired.

GUNFIRE ON THE RANCH

USA TODAY Bestselling Author

DELORES FOSSEN

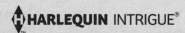

Recycling programs
for this product may
not exist in your area.

ISBN-13: 978-1-335-63889-2

Gunfire on the Ranch

Copyright © 2017 by Delores Fossen

Printed in U.S.A.

Delores Fossen, a *USA TODAY* bestselling author, has sold over fifty novels, with millions of copies of her books in print worldwide. She's received a Booksellers' Best Award and an RT Reviewers' Choice Best Book Award. She was also a finalist for a prestigious RITA® Award. You can contact the author through her website at www.deloresfossen.com.

Books by Delores Fossen

Harlequin Intrigue

Blue River Ranch

Always a Lawman
Gunfire on the Ranch

The Lawmen of Silver Creek Ranch

Grayson
Dade
Nate
Kade
Gage
Mason
Josh
Sawyer
Landon
Holden

HQN Books

The McCord Brothers

What Happens on the Ranch
(ebook novella)
Texas on My Mind
Cowboy Trouble
(ebook novella)
Lone Star Nights
Cowboy Underneath It All
(ebook novella)
Blame It on the Cowboy

A Wrangler's Creek Novel

Lone Star Cowboy
(ebook novella)
Those Texas Nights
One Good Cowboy
(ebook novella)
No Getting Over a Cowboy
Just Like a Cowboy
(ebook novella)
Branded as Trouble

Visit the Author Profile page at Harlequin.com.

CAST OF CHARACTERS

DEA agent Theo Canton—Ten years ago he left his hometown, but after hearing a hit man has targeted his old flame, Ivy Beckett, Theo returns to the Blue River Ranch to protect her. He soon learns Ivy has been keeping a secret from him.

Ivy Beckett—After her parents were brutally murdered and Theo and she parted ways, Ivy, too, left Blue River. Her return was supposed to be a short one, to attend her brother's wedding, but it becomes a dangerous nightmare for Ivy and her son.

Nathan Beckett—Ivy's nine-year-old son, who could get caught in the crosshairs of a killer.

Wesley Sanford—Theo's fellow DEA agent who volunteers to help him find the person who's trying to kill Ivy, but Wesley might have his own agenda.

Lacey Vogel—Ivy's adult stepdaughter. She's furious that her late father left his estate to Ivy and not her. Just how far would she go to get back at Ivy?

August Canton—Theo's uncle. His brother, Travis, is in jail for murdering Ivy's parents, and August would do anything to clear his brother's name.

Sheriff Gabriel Beckett—He's not only the head of Blue River Ranch, he's also the law in his hometown, and he has no intention of letting a killer get to his sister—or allowing Theo to break her heart again.

Chapter One

Theo Canton wished there was a better way to stop a killer. Anything other than coming here to the Beckett Ranch to disrupt wedding plans. But if his intel was right, there could be another murder—tonight.

Maybe Ivy Beckett's murder.

Hell, maybe her entire family and Theo's sister, since they would possibly all be under the same roof for the ceremony. A ceremony that was to take place tomorrow.

Theo definitely didn't want a repeat of what had happened ten years ago when two people died at the hands of a killer. Just the thought of it put a knot in his stomach, along with bringing back old memories. He had to shove those memories aside, though, because they would only cause him to lose focus.

He had enough Beckett blood on his hands without adding more.

Theo took the final turn to the ranch and spotted the decorations already on the pasture fences. Blue satin ribbon flapping in the hot May breeze. There were no ranch hands out and about. No signs of a killer, either, but the snake could already be there, waiting to strike.

His phone buzzed, and he saw the name flash on the screen. Wesley Sanford, a fellow DEA agent who'd alerted Theo that there could be a problem, that a killer could be headed to the ranch. Theo kept his attention on the road, on his surroundings, too, but he hit the answer button to put the call on speaker.

"Anything?" Wesley asked right away.

"No, not yet. How about you?"

"I'll be at the Blue River sheriff's office in just a couple of minutes. I'll tell the deputies what's going on. I might even get the chance to speak to Gabriel himself."

Gabriel, the sheriff of the ranching town of Blue River as well as Ivy's brother. Well, one of them, anyway. Her other brother, Jameson, was a Texas Ranger.

"But I'm guessing that the sheriff won't be

working this late the night before his wedding?" Wesley added.

Theo had no idea. He hadn't kept up with
news on the Becketts. They were more of
those old memories, and wounds, that he
hadn't wanted in his life. Besides, the Becketts wouldn't want him keeping up with them.
Or even want him around, for that matter.
They'd made that crystal clear ten years ago.
Theo had had no choice but to come tonight,
though. Once the danger was over, however,
he'd get out of there as fast as he had a decade ago.

"If Gabriel is at his office," Theo told Wesley, "remember not to say anything in the police station. Take him outside to talk." If their
criminal informant had been right, the killer
could have managed to plant a bug in the
building. And in the sheriff's house. "I don't
want this clown to know we're onto him. I
want to catch him."

Wesley hadn't especially needed that reminder, but the stakes were too high for either of them to make a mistake. The last time
Theo had made a mistake with the Becketts,
Ivy's parents had been murdered. Maybe by
this same killer who was after them now.

Or maybe by Theo's own father.

But if his father had actually been the murderer ten years ago, then tonight Theo was dealing with a copycat. Because his father was miles away behind bars in a maximum-security prison. Still, a copycat could be just as lethal as the original one had been.

Too bad Theo couldn't just sound the alarm and alert Ivy's brothers and the ranch hands, but that possible bug in Gabriel's house meant the only secure way for Theo to contact the Becketts was outside, face-to-face.

"Whether the sheriff is here or not, I'll let someone know there might be a bug," Wesley assured him. "Call me when you can."

Theo hit the end-call button on his phone just as he reached the top of the hill, and the ranch house came into view. Well, one of the houses, anyway. From what he'd learned, there were now four on the grounds. One for Gabriel. Another belonging to Jameson. The third was one Gabriel's deputy and longtime friend, Cameron Doran, had built.

It was the fourth house, though, that contained the bad memories.

Because that was where Ivy's parents had been murdered. No one lived there and hadn't since, well, since that night.

According to the quick check Theo had

done before he'd left for Blue River, Ivy's house was hours away in a rural area near Houston. Apparently, Theo wasn't the only one who'd left Blue River after the murders.

Other than her address, there hadn't been a lot of info to find on Ivy, though she had listed herself as widowed on the tax documents for her small ranch. So she'd not only moved on physically but also emotionally with another man she'd married and lost. Theo felt a hit of the jealousy before he quickly reined it in. Ivy wasn't his, hadn't been for a long time, so of course she had moved on. That's what normal people did.

Theo hadn't considered himself *normal* in a while now.

He stopped his truck beneath a cluster of trees only about twenty yards from Gabriel's house. Theo drew his gun and made his way to the side of the wraparound porch. There were plenty of shrubs where he could hide and have a line of sight to all four houses. However, he'd barely gotten into position when he heard something he didn't want to hear.

"Drop your gun," someone snapped.

Hell. How had a person managed to get so close without him noticing? And it wasn't just any ordinary someone, either. Theo recognized that voice even after all these years.

Ivy.

He turned, slowly, and he spotted her at the back corner of the house. Thanks to the light coming from one of the windows, he had no trouble seeing her face.

And the rifle she was pointing at him.

Apparently, she had no trouble seeing him, either, because she whispered his name on a rise of breath. What she didn't do was lower her weapon.

Theo said her name, and it had far more emotion in it than he wanted. Of course, any drop of emotion was too much right now, since he didn't want their past playing into this. She was his ex-lover, emphasis on the *ex*. All he wanted now was to do his job and get the heck out of there.

Ivy didn't say anything else, but she started walking toward him. Her attention volleyed between his face and his gun, which he lowered to his side.

"I was getting something from Gabriel's office when I glanced out the window and saw you," she finally said. "We didn't expect you. Judging from the way you were sneaking around, you didn't want us to see you."

No, he hadn't wanted the killer to see him.

"I had to come," he told her. "I found out… something."

Ivy flinched a little and came even closer until she was only about a foot away from him. She hadn't changed much in the past ten years. She was almost thirty now and still had that thick, dark brown hair that fell just past her shoulders. Still had the same intense eyes. He couldn't see the color of them in the darkness, but he knew they were sapphire blue.

Despite Theo's not wanting to feel anything, he did. The old attraction that for some stupid reason felt just as strong as it always had. But he was also feeling something else. The anger. That's why he kept watch around them.

"I guess you heard about the wedding. Are you here to see your sister?" she asked.

"No." Best not to get into the fact that he hadn't seen his kid sister, Jodi, in a long time. Because that was a different set of bad memories. Not because he didn't love her. He did. But Jodi was a reminder that he'd failed her, too. She'd nearly gotten killed the same night as Ivy's folks, and he hadn't been able to stop it. Now, all these years later, she was marrying Gabriel Beckett.

So obviously Gabriel and Jodi had managed

to work through their shared painful pasts. He guessed they'd found their "normal."

"It's not safe for us to be out here," Theo explained. "We need to get in my truck so we can talk."

She didn't budge, but she did follow his gaze when he looked around again. "You heard about the threatening letter," Ivy said.

No, he hadn't, but it got his attention, and Theo shook his head. "What letter?"

Ivy huffed, and she finally lowered her gun. "The latest one had a warning that my brothers, my sister and I would all be murdered on the anniversary of our parents' deaths."

Which was only two months away.

Ivy's tone practically dismissed the threat her family had gotten. But Theo wasn't dismissing anything. "You get a lot of letters like that?"

"Enough. Emails, too, and the occasional phone call from blocked numbers. If you didn't know about that, then why are you here?" she asked without hesitating. "And why did you say it wasn't safe for us to be out here?"

"Because it's not." He took a deep breath. "You know I'm a special agent in the DEA?"

Her mouth tightened, and she nodded. "Gabriel says you're what law enforcement calls a joe."

That was the slang term for it all right. An agent who went into deep cover, sometimes years at a time. Just as Theo had done. In fact, he was less than a month out of a three-year assignment where he'd infiltrated a militia group to track the sale of drugs.

"Yes," he verified, "and I have access to criminal informants who give me intel from time to time. According to one of those informants, there's a killer coming here to the ranch tonight."

Her eyes widened. Then narrowed just as fast. She looked ready to bolt, of course, but he saw her quickly rein that in. "How reliable is this so-called intel?"

Good question. "Reliable enough for me to come to a place where I know I'm not welcome."

She stayed quiet a moment. "You could have just called," Ivy pointed out, confirming his notion about his not being welcome.

He shook his head. "According to the informant, the killer managed to bug both the sheriff's office and Gabriel's house."

Theo saw another punch of concern on her face, maybe some skepticism, too, and she had another look around as Theo did. "This killer is connected to my parents' murders?"

"The informant says the killer is." Theo paused. "But the informant also said this is the same guy who murdered your folks."

Ivy groaned. Mumbled some profanity under her breath. "We know who killed them. Your father, Travis Canton. And he's sitting in jail right now because there was more than enough evidence to prove he'd done it."

No, there was more than enough evidence to *convict* him. That was splitting hairs, but since his father couldn't remember if he'd murdered the Becketts, Theo still had his doubts.

"Travis hated my parents," Ivy reminded him as if he'd said those doubts aloud. "He threatened them just hours before the murders. And when the deputies found him by the creek, he had my father's blood on his shirt."

All of that was true. What she could have added was that Travis was an alcoholic who'd experienced blackouts, both that night and others. He could have killed the Becketts in a drunken haze and not even remembered.

Or someone could have set him up.

Someone waiting to finish the job by killing the Becketts' children.

"Your father was the sheriff at the time of his murder," he continued. What he was about to say would be old news to her, but he wanted to remind her that everything might not be black-and-white here. "Your mother was a former cop. They had plenty of enemies because of the arrests they made over the years. One of those enemies could be coming after you tonight, and that's why you don't need to be standing out here."

There was a bit more worry in her eyes this time when she glanced around. But she still didn't budge.

Now it was Theo's turn to mumble some profanity. "Look, I know Gabriel, Jameson and your sister, Lauren, won't want me inside—"

"Lauren's not here and won't be coming. She left town around the same time you did and hasn't been back."

Theo couldn't fault her for that. Lauren was the youngest, had been barely eighteen when she'd been made an orphan. Like Theo, she had no doubt wanted a fresh start.

"I'm sorry," he said, because it sounded as if Ivy was hurt that Lauren wasn't there. It was a hurt he understood. "Hell, maybe my own sister won't want me here, either. But can we at least sit in my truck while I convince you that this threat could be real?"

"And how will you do that?" she asked. Yeah, he'd been right about that skepticism.

"I've got a recording from the criminal informant. He knew some things about the night of the murders. Things that weren't revealed to the press. He says the killer told him those things."

Her attention slashed toward the house. "Gabriel will need to hear this." And now there was some urgency in her voice.

Yes, he would. Jameson, too. And Jodi. "But not inside. Remember, there could be listening devices. If the killer knows we're onto him, it could send him back underground where he could prepare for another attack. And next time, we might not get a heads-up from a CI."

He could see the debate going on inside her, and with each passing second, Theo's unease escalated. It really wasn't a smart idea for them to be outside.

"Your brothers don't trust me," he added. "I get that."

Man, did he. Because for a short period of time after the Becketts were murdered, Theo had been a suspect.

His father wasn't the only one who'd had bad blood with Ivy's parents.

Just hours before their murder, Theo had had a run-in with Ivy's father, Sherman, and Sherman had told him in no uncertain terms that he was to stop seeing Ivy, that she didn't need a bad boy in her life. Theo had been furious, even though Sherman had been right—Ivy had deserved something better.

"Yes," Ivy whispered as if she knew exactly what he was thinking. "But let's not allow old water and old bridges to play into this. Gabriel needs to hear this recording and decide if it's something we should be worried about."

Yes, and her brother *would* be worried once he heard what the CI had to say.

Ivy motioned for him to follow her. Not to his truck but rather to the back of the house. She hurried, thank God, which meant it had finally sunk in that she was in danger. But since she was clearly taking him inside, Theo had to speak up.

"Remember the part about a possible bug. When we're inside, whisper." That might not be enough if the listening device was sensitive and had a wide range, but at this point he just wanted her out of the line of possible fire.

She led him onto the porch and through

the back door, but Ivy stopped in a mudroom, where there were raincoats on wall pegs and cowboy boots stashed beside a wooden bench. A reminder that this was indeed a working ranch. Gabriel wasn't just a sheriff, but also raised cattle and horses. There were cans of paint and what appeared to be scaffolding, as well.

"There was a fire last month," Ivy said, following his gaze. "An attack. That's why I want to make sure another one doesn't happen."

He wanted the same thing, especially since Theo had read about that attack. His sister had been the target, and even though the guy was now dead, he'd clearly left his mark.

"I'll have Gabriel come back here." Ivy put the rifle on the top shelf of the storage closet, took out her phone from her jeans pocket and sent off a text.

Theo had another look around, shut the back door and then glanced out the single window that was in the small room. Ivy reached for the light switch to turn it on, but he stopped her. Of course, that meant touching her, and he got another sucker punch of the old heat.

A third sucker punch when their gazes met.

She didn't say anything, but Theo thought maybe she had felt it, too. He also thought maybe she was fighting to push it away as hard as he was. Yes, she was a widow, but after everything they'd gone through, she probably didn't want to have another round with him any more than he did with her.

"It's not a good idea to be this close to a window," Theo insisted. And yes, he whispered. "We should at least get down."

She clamped her teeth over her bottom lip for a couple of seconds. A gesture he'd seen her do so many times. Nerves. But she finally ducked down so that her head wouldn't be anywhere near the glass. Theo ducked, too, but he stayed high enough so he could continue to glance out and make sure the killer wasn't sneaking up on them.

The moments crawled by, and with each one of them Theo became well aware of the close contact between them. It was hard to fight the attraction and the old memories when they were this close. And when he caught her scent.

Hell.

For just a split second, the image of her naked body flashed into his head.

Thankfully, the image didn't stay. It vanished when he heard the voice and the sound of footsteps. It was yet another voice he recognized. Gabriel's.

Theo braced himself for whatever Gabriel might dole out. He could just order Theo out of there, but Gabriel barely spared him a glance when he stepped into the doorway. That's because he was on his phone, and he took his sister by the arm and moved her out of the mudroom and into the adjacent kitchen.

Once Gabriel had done that, he finished his call, slipped his phone back into his jeans pocket and finally looked at Theo. This time, it was more than a glance.

"What the hell did you do? Who did you bring with you?" Gabriel demanded. But he didn't give Theo a chance to answer. "One of the ranch hands just called. He spotted an armed man crawling over the back fence, and the man's making his way to the house right now."

Chapter Two

Ivy's heart slammed against her chest. She had already been feeling so many emotions, including dread and fear, but this was a different kind of fear.

There's a killer coming here to the ranch tonight.

She hadn't exactly dismissed Theo's warning, but Ivy had prayed he was wrong. Apparently not, though. Because she doubted an armed intruder had good intentions. And according to Gabriel, he was on his way to the house. Ivy would have bolted toward the front stairs if Gabriel hadn't taken hold of her arm again.

"I've already told the others to lock up and get down," her brother said. "They're fine." He slapped off the kitchen lights and tipped his head to the back door where Theo and she had entered. "Lock that," he added to Theo. Theo did, and Gabriel used his phone to arm the security system.

"There could be listening devices planted in the house and at your office." Theo hurried into the kitchen with them. "Who else is here?" Theo asked at the same moment that Gabriel threw out a question of his own.

"What do you have to do with the armed guy?"

Judging from the glare Gabriel aimed at Theo, her brother felt his question had priority over Theo's. Theo must have felt the same way, because he started talking.

"I don't know who he is, but I have a recording of a CI who says that a killer is on the way to the ranch. I didn't call because supposedly this killer had managed to plant bugs in the house and the sheriff's office, and I didn't want to tip him off that we were onto him. But obviously we're past the point of being worried about tipping him off."

"Yeah." A muscle flickered in Gabriel's jaw. "How long had Theo been here before you texted me?" he asked her.

"Just a few seconds." That was possibly true. Ivy honestly had no idea how long it'd been. Time had sort of frozen when she'd come face-to-face with the man she'd never expected to see again.

Gabriel stared at her as if he might challenge that, but then he growled out, "Follow me."

Ivy was certain that put some renewed panic in her eyes, certain that her brother saw it as well, but Gabriel kept moving, anyway. "We'll go into my office."

Not upstairs. Though that's where Ivy wanted to go. "Nathan," she said.

"He's in the guest room with Jameson and Jodi," Gabriel quickly answered. "They moved him into the bathroom and will make sure he's all right."

That steadied Ivy a little. Jameson was a lawman, and Jodi had been trained as a private security specialist. Still, Ivy didn't want a gunman anywhere near the house or anyone in her family.

"Nathan?" Theo asked.

"Ivy's son," Gabriel said before she could answer. "If this gunman makes it to the house, he'll be seriously outnumbered. But it might not even come to that, because I have three armed ranch hands headed out to stop him."

Gabriel must have made those arrangements shortly before he'd come to the mudroom. Good. Ivy wanted every precaution taken. Correction: she *needed* it, because she had to keep Nathan safe.

"You have a son?" Theo asked, his voice practically a whisper now.

"Yes." She didn't give any other details. No time. Because Gabriel spoke again.

"I want to know everything about the recording," Gabriel insisted, glancing at Theo again. "I want to hear what this CI has to say."

Theo nodded and followed Gabriel into his office, which was just off the family room on the bottom floor. There were plenty of windows here, but Gabriel had already shut the blinds and drapes. He also didn't turn on the lights. No doubt because it would alert anyone close enough to the house that there was someone in that particular room.

However, her brother did go to one of the windows that faced the back of the house, and he opened the blinds just enough so he could keep watch. Theo did the same to the window across from Gabriel. That one would give him a view of the side of the house. While the inside of the house was practically dark, there were security lights on the grounds, so maybe they'd be able to see this monster coming.

"Is there an extra gun in here?" Ivy asked.

"Bottom right drawer," Gabriel quickly provided. It was locked, but he rattled off the combination, and she took out a Glock he had stashed there. She wasn't an expert marksman, not by any stretch of the imagination, but she would use it to defend her son if necessary.

"The CI is someone who regularly gives me intel," Theo started. "I'll write down his name for you later. In case the place really is bugged, I don't want to compromise his identity. The other person you'll hear on the recording is a federal agent. He's the one who sent me this, and the voices have been altered—again so that no one will be compromised."

While still keeping a grip on his gun, Theo took out his phone and hit the play button. He held it up so that Gabriel would be able to hear it, and it didn't take long before the man's voice began to pour through the room.

"I heard some stuff," the man said. "Stuff about them Becketts. I figured I oughta tell you because that family's been through enough."

Yes, they had been. The murder of their parents. Also the near murder of Gabriel's bride-to-be, Jodi. It had changed their lives forever.

It was still changing them.

"There's a killer coming after them," the man went on. "I don't know the fella's name, but I heard him talking at the Silver Moon Bar over on St. Mary's Street. He said he'd been hired—and these are his words, not mine—*to put some more Becketts in the ground.* He said he was going to the Blue River Ranch tonight to finish off as many of them as he could."

A chill slid through Ivy, head to toe, and she felt her stomach clench into a tight knot. "God, will this never end?" she said under her breath.

Ivy clearly hadn't said that softly enough, because it caused both Theo and her brother to look back at her. Theo hit Pause. He stared at her as if he might need to intervene in some way. Definitely not something she wanted. Nor did she want to give in to the fear. So she went to the window next to Theo in order to help him keep watch.

Theo continued to look at her while he volleyed glances out the window, but he finally hit the play button again.

"Describe the man who said that." It was a second person on the recording. Theo's fellow agent, no doubt. "And did he say who hired him?"

"Didn't mention a word about that," the CI answered. "Of course, it wouldn't have been too smart if he had. And I couldn't exactly ask him without maybe gettin' my own self killed. But he was tall, bulky. Built like one of those navy SEALs or something."

Theo looked at Gabriel then, and her brother nodded. "That matches the description of the man the ranch hand saw."

"How do you know this hired gun is for real?" the agent asked the CI.

"'Cause he knew things, that's why. Things about Sheriff Sherman Beckett and his wife, Millie, who got killed ten years ago. It was all over the news, but this fella told me there was something the news didn't mention. Something that the cops kept out of the papers. He said the killer took Sherman Beckett's watch. Pulled it right off his dead wrist. And that he took Millie's necklace. It was a heart-shaped locket and had pictures of her kids in it."

It was true. All true. Those items had indeed been missing, though they hadn't been found on the killer, Theo's father, Travis. Ivy had always assumed that Travis had dropped them or hidden them somewhere, but how would this man have known that?

That didn't help the knot in her stomach, and Ivy had to fight to hang on to what little composure she had left. She had prayed this was all some kind of misunderstanding, that the CI had been wrong, but apparently no such luck. There really was a killer headed to the house who had plans to finish them all off.

"Did this hired gun say anything else?" the agent pressed. "Anything that would help us figure out who's paying him to do this?"

"Nope, but I figure it's gotta be Travis Canton. Yeah, I know he's in jail, but something like this could get him out from behind bars."

Theo didn't say anything, but even in the near darkness, she saw his jaw tighten. "I've already checked with the prison," Theo volunteered, "and other than his lawyer, my father hasn't had any visitors in the past week. Plus, he doesn't have the funds to hire a hit man."

So maybe this was the work of some kind of psycho groupie. There'd been so much interest in the murders, partly because Jodi had also been attacked and left for dead in a shallow grave. And all that interest had attracted some very sick people.

"I know you gotta tell this to the Becketts," the CI went on a moment later, "but you oughta be careful when you do it. The fella at the bar said he'd put bugs in the sheriff's place and his house. So if you say anything to them, sure as hell don't mention my name. I don't want that SOB comin' after me."

"That's the end of the conversation," Theo told them. "But you can see why I had to come."

Yes, she could. Since the CI had been right about the hired killer, maybe he was right about that bug, too. It sickened her to think that someone had been spying on them, listening to their every word. Someone who now wanted to kill them.

Her brother must have realized that, too, because he cursed and fired off a text. Several seconds later, his phone buzzed. He set it aside and put it on speaker, no doubt to keep his hands free for his gun.

"Sorry, Gabriel," the caller immediately said. It was Aiken Colley, one of Gabriel's ranch hands. "But we lost sight of the guy."

That was not what Ivy wanted to hear, and she made a frantic search of every part of the grounds that she could see. No signs of a gunman. No signs of anyone.

Gabriel cursed. "Where was he when you last saw him?"

"By the south barn."

That wasn't that far from the house. Worse, there were other outbuildings and fences between the house and that particular barn, and this man could use those to conceal himself so he could get closer.

"I never had a clean shot of him," Aiken went on. "The guy was running, and every few seconds, he would duck behind cover. Jake and Teddy are out here with me, and I've alerted the other hands."

Jake and Teddy were two other hands, and while none of the hands were in law enforcement, they all knew how to handle guns. But apparently this hired killer knew how to dodge those guns.

"If possible, I want this guy alive," Theo said.

Gabriel didn't disagree with that. Probably because a dead man couldn't give them answers, but at the moment Ivy cared only about keeping this monster away from Nathan and everyone else in the house.

"Kill him only if necessary. And be careful," Gabriel warned the ranch hand.

"We will. We'll keep looking for him until we find him," Aiken added before he ended the call.

Ivy got back to keeping watch. Not that she hadn't been doing that, but she adjusted her position just enough so that she could try to take in more of the yard and the pastures. Still no sign of him, but she could almost feel him closing in on them.

Who the heck was putting this monster up to this?

The CI had said it was Travis, and perhaps it was. Maybe he'd somehow gotten the money. But there was also another possibility. One that had been a thorn in her family's side since Travis had first been arrested.

"Could your uncle August be behind this?" Ivy asked Theo. "Because August has been adamant that Travis is innocent."

August was Travis's half brother. A hothead. In the past ten years, he'd never turned to violence to free his brother, but August could be getting desperate since Travis had exhausted all his appeals.

"I haven't spoken to August since I left Blue River," Theo answered. "I tried to call him, but he didn't answer. If he had anything to do with this, I'll deal with him."

Judging from Theo's tone, that would not be pleasant. Not a surprise. There was no love lost between Jodi and their uncle, and it appeared to be the same for Theo. Of course, that was probably because August was not an easy man to like, and he was always saying that Travis's "ungrateful kids" weren't doing enough to help their father.

Theo's phone buzzed. "It's the agent who recorded the conversation with the CI," Theo relayed to them, but he didn't mention the guy by name. However, as Gabriel had done, he put the call on speaker. "The gunman's here," Theo told the agent right off. "Not in the house, but it appears this is where he's headed."

The agent didn't jump to answer. It seemed as if he took a moment to process that. "You want me out there?"

"Not yet. This goon could fire shots at you as you drive up. Plus, I don't want to send him running."

Part of Ivy wanted him to run. To get as far away from Nathan as possible. But Theo was right. If the guy ran, he could possibly just regroup and come back for a second attempt.

"Did you find any bugs in the sheriff's office?" Theo asked.

"Not yet, but the deputies are looking. One of them spoke to Gabriel a little while ago. He stepped outside to do that."

"Cameron," Gabriel provided. "He called the moment the agent showed up at the office."

Of course he had. He wouldn't have kept

Gabriel in the dark about something this big. That meant Gabriel had been plenty busy in the short time since all of this mess had started with Theo's arrival.

"The deputy wants to know if you need backup," the agent continued.

"Not yet," Gabriel answered before Theo could say anything. "But keep watch, because there might be more than one hired gun. Whoever's behind this could have sent someone there."

Oh, mercy. She hadn't even considered that. But if someone had indeed wanted to put the Becketts "in the grave," then the person might have gone looking for Gabriel at work.

"I just got a call," the agent continued. "The CI is dead."

Other than hearing she had a son, Theo hadn't seemed surprised by much of what had happened. But he was clearly surprised now. And riled. "How the hell did that happen?"

"We're not sure yet. We had a tail on him, just in case he tried to follow the hired gun or something, but the tail stayed a safe distance back. He saw someone dressed all in black gun the guy down."

Ivy doubted that was a coincidence, and that meant… Oh, God.

"Was this all a setup?" she asked. Neither Gabriel nor Theo jumped to deny that, and that only caused her heart to pound even harder. "You think the hired gun wanted Theo to come here?" she added.

Again, they didn't deny it. "If so, it worked," Gabriel mumbled, and he tacked on some profanity.

Yes, it had. But what did it mean? It didn't take Ivy long to come up with something that she didn't want to consider.

All the "survivors" of the murders were now under the same roof. Gabriel, Jameson, Jodi, Theo and her. Along with their sister, Lauren, all five of them had been either in the house where her parents were murdered or on the grounds. Which meant they had all been possible witnesses to the crime.

Possible, but they actually hadn't been.

Ivy had been in her upstairs bedroom with her headphones on. And crying. Because of the blowup that Theo had just had with her folks. The music had been so loud that she hadn't heard her mother and father being murdered in the room just below her. Some people had told her that it was a blessing she hadn't heard because if she had, she would have gone downstairs and possibly been killed, too. But

Ivy wished she had heard. Because she might have been able to save them.

Jodi hadn't heard the murders going on, either. She'd been outside, coming back from Gabriel's house, which was a short distance away. She'd been attacked that night. Not by the killer, though. But rather by her ex-boyfriend who'd been in a rage over their breakup. Since he was now dead, he was no longer a possible witness.

Jameson and Gabriel had been at their own houses, but they were close enough to the main ranch house that they could have seen something. They hadn't. But maybe the killer hadn't known or believed that.

"What could your father or August possibly hope to gain by eliminating witnesses?" Ivy came out and asked.

"They wouldn't," Theo answered.

She looked at Gabriel to see if he would argue that. He didn't. "If they wanted to clear Travis's name," Gabriel explained, "they could be desperate enough to arrange a murder. But Theo and Jodi wouldn't be the targets."

Because Travis still seemingly loved his children. Of course, that didn't exclude Travis's brother. August wasn't fond of Jodi or

Theo. "This could all be something August put together."

"If August had come up with this plan to make my father look innocent," Theo went on, "he would have hired someone to stab his victim."

The way her parents had been killed.

Ivy was about to say that could be the hired thug's plan. But then she heard a sound that stopped her cold.

"Get down!" someone shouted. Aiken.

But there was no time to do that. Because a bullet came crashing through the window where Ivy was standing.

Chapter Three

Hell. Theo hadn't even seen the shot coming.

But he sure as heck heard it. Felt it, too, when the glass flew through the room and a piece of it sliced across his cheek. It stung, but he ignored it and scrambled toward Ivy so he could pull her to the floor. She had already started in that direction, but Theo helped her along by hooking his arm around her and dragging her about five feet away from the window.

Good thing, because another bullet tore through what was left of the glass.

"Stay down," Theo warned her, and he put her behind a huge leather chair so he could hurry back to the window. He didn't get directly in front of it but instead kept to the side.

This was exactly what Theo had been trying to stop. Ivy and her family had been through enough, but apparently that moron outside didn't feel the same. He was adding to their misery, and in doing so, he was putting an innocent child in danger. Theo didn't know how old Nathan was, but it was possible he was a baby.

"Do you see him?" Gabriel asked. He came to the window next to Theo and peered out through the edge of the blinds.

Theo looked over the grounds as best he could, but there were too many places their attacker could use for cover. A barn, several vehicles, shrubs and trees. However, it became a little easier to narrow down a hiding place when the next shot blasted through the air. Like the other two, this one slammed into the wall near the door, and it allowed Theo to pinpoint the man's location.

"He's on the right side of the barn," Theo relayed to Gabriel. "I can't see him, but I can see a rifle barrel."

Gabriel didn't waste any time. He tossed Ivy his phone. "Text Aiken and tell him to stay back from the barn." And like Theo, Gabriel took aim in that direction.

Theo didn't look back at Ivy, but he could hear the clicks on the phone as she wrote. However, they were soon drowned out by another shot. This time, it went through the window near Gabriel.

That must have been the final straw for Ivy's brother because he cursed, took aim at the barn and fired. Theo did the same, all the while watching to see if their attacker would show his face. He didn't. And he didn't seem put off by being shot at, because he continued to fire, as well. However, something was off because Theo could no longer see the rifle.

"I think he's trying to make a getaway," Theo mumbled. "I'll go after him." He didn't allow Gabriel or Ivy a say in that. Keeping low, Theo hurried toward the door. "Disarm the security system so I can go out front but reset it as soon as I'm outside."

Theo had only been in Gabriel's house a time or two even though the man had lived there for going on thirteen years. Gabriel hadn't exactly been a fan of Theo's when he'd been dating Ivy, but Theo had dropped by a couple of times to pick her up there. That's why Theo knew the general layout, and he ran up the hall and through the family room to get to the front door.

Gabriel must have turned off the system because the alarm didn't go off when Theo eased open the door. However, he did hear a sound he didn't especially want to hear.

Footsteps behind him.

It was Gabriel. "You'll need help," Gabriel growled.

"You should stay with Ivy," Theo growled right back.

"She's the one who insisted I go with you." Gabriel didn't seem especially pleased about that.

This was part of that "old water, old bridge" thing between Theo and the Becketts. Still, Gabriel was a lawman, and he knew it was a stupid time to discuss this or anything else, especially all that old baggage. Gabriel rearmed the security system, this time using the keypad on the wall, and he shut the door. He then tipped his head to the left side of the house.

"I'll go that way," Gabriel said, "and make my way to the back. As soon as I get to the porch, I'll fire at the barn, but I'll keep my shots low to try to avoid a kill shot. You do the same from this side of the house. Ivy's texting the hands to let them know we're out here so they won't hit us by mistake."

Good. Gabriel had been thorough. Now, if everything played out as planned, they could catch this snake and get him to talk. If August or his father was involved, then there'd be hell to pay. Not just from Theo but from the Becketts.

Theo made his way to the side of the porch and peered around the edge. He was careful, but the gunman must have been looking for him because he sent a shot right at Theo. It smashed into the wood siding, tearing a hole in it.

That caused Theo to curse again, and he hoped like the devil that none of those shots made it through the wall where Ivy was or upstairs to the others. If the shots went in the direction of her son, Theo was almost certain that Ivy would go running up there, and in doing so she might get herself killed.

Theo waited, giving Gabriel a couple of seconds to get into place, and even though those seconds seemed to crawl by, he knew Gabriel was hurrying. And the next sound Theo heard was a shot coming from the direction where Gabriel had said he would be. Their attacker would obviously soon know that Gabriel was back there.

Theo leaned out, aiming low, and he fired two rounds. Almost immediately, he ducked back behind cover. Good thing, too, because the gunman fired off two rounds of his own at

Theo. But Theo could also hear the man cursing. Maybe because he'd been hit. Perhaps because he realized that coming here alone had been a stupid mistake.

That last thought had no sooner crossed his mind when Theo felt that bad feeling crawl up his spine. It was a feeling that had saved his butt a few times, so he didn't ignore it. He pivoted, looking around him.

And spotted the second man near Theo's own truck.

He was dressed all in black, armed with multiple weapons on an equipment belt. He had one weapon in his hand, as well. That's the one he aimed at Theo.

Theo fired first.

He double tapped the trigger, the shots slamming directly into the man's chest, and the guy dropped to the ground. Maybe dead or dying, but it was equally possible that he was wearing a Kevlar vest and had simply had the breath knocked out of him. If so, he could still be dangerous.

"There's a second gunman," Theo called out to Gabriel. "And there might be others."

Of course, Gabriel didn't need him to add that last part, but it was also, hopefully, a reminder for everyone inside to stay down. Especially Ivy. She was on the bottom floor and could easily be hit by bullets meant for Gabriel and him.

The guy by the barn fired another couple of shots, one of them in Theo's direction. At least one went toward Gabriel's office, though. Maybe the guy had thermal equipment or something because he seemed to know that there was still someone in that particular room. When the goon sent another shot at the office, Theo knew he couldn't wait.

He leaned out and fired.

Not low this time.

Theo sent some rounds in the area of the shooter's chest. And finally the shots stopped. Just like that, it was quiet again. Theo didn't hear any moaning or sounds of pain. Definitely didn't hear anyone trying to run away.

It was a risk. Anything he did at this point could be, but Theo left the porch and ran toward his truck, where the second gunman was still on the ground. He kept his gun ready, kept watch around him, too, but as he approached the man, he didn't see any movement.

But he did see blood.

It was on the ground around the guy, which meant he hadn't been wearing Kevlar after all. Theo touched his fingers to the man's neck.

Dead.

He didn't curse, though that's what he wanted to do. Maybe the other one was still alive.

Using shrubs for cover, Theo started making his way to the barn. "I'm back here," he called out to Gabriel.

But calling out to him wasn't necessary because Theo soon spotted the sheriff at the back of the house. Gabriel was closer to the barn now, heading toward the first gunman. And he wasn't alone. There was another man with Gabriel. One of the hands no doubt.

"Are the hired killers dead?" Ivy asked, and that's when Theo realized she was at one of the blasted-out windows.

"Get down!" Theo ordered her.

He hurried past Ivy but not before he got a glimpse of her face. She was too pale and had a death grip on the gun she'd taken from her brother's desk, but she appeared to be unharmed. Physically, anyway. This had to be triggering flashbacks of her parents' murders. Also triggering new fears of the danger to her son and family.

Gabriel and the hand got to the gunman ahead of Theo, and Theo braced himself for Gabriel to say the guy was dead. He didn't.

"Ivy, call an ambulance," Gabriel shouted. "Tell the medics to hurry."

Theo soon figured out why the hurry part was necessary. Just like the guy in the front yard, this one had gunshots to the chest, and he was bleeding out fast. Theo kicked away the guy's weapon just as Gabriel got right in the man's face.

"Who hired you?" Gabriel demanded, sounding very much like the lawman that he was.

The guy shook his head, and he opened his mouth as if to answer. But he didn't. His eyelids drifted down, and his head flopped back, prompting Gabriel to check for a pulse.

"He's still alive," Gabriel said, glancing at Theo. "Go back in and check on Ivy and the others. Ivy still has my phone so tell her to disarm the security system. Also let Jameson know what's going on."

Theo didn't like leaving Gabriel out there with just the hand, but he soon saw two other men making their way toward them. Not gunmen. These were dressed like ranch hands.

"I heard Gabriel," Ivy volunteered. Which meant she was still too close to the blasted window. "I turned off the alarm."

Good, because the sooner Theo got in the house, the sooner he could chew her out for taking a risk like standing too close to the window. But he didn't get a chance to even start the chewing out. By the time he was through the door and into the foyer, Ivy was already headed up the stairs. Theo shut the door and followed her.

She stopped at the top of the stairs, looked at him, and he saw that her bottom lip was trembling. Actually, she was trembling all over.

"There really could be others?" she asked. Her voice was as shaky as the rest of her.

"Maybe." And he hated that he even had to say that to her because it certainly didn't help with her frayed nerves. "We just don't know who or what we're dealing with right now."

She nodded. But didn't budge. "I need a second to calm down. I don't want Nathan to see me like this."

Theo understood that. As a single mom, she probably wanted to be strong for her kid. But she took more than a second, and the trembling seemed to be getting worse. He figured it was a mistake, but since Theo didn't know what the heck else to do, he put his arm around her.

Ivy automatically stiffened. Maybe because the last time she'd been in his arms, they'd still been lovers. But there was no trace of that attraction now, and Theo heard her try to choke back a sob.

She pulled away from him, hiking up her chin. Or rather, trying. She wasn't doing a very good job of it until one of the doors opened and Jameson stuck out his head.

"Are you okay?" Jameson asked, his attention going straight to his sister.

She gave another nod. "Gabriel's with one of the gunmen, the one who's still alive. The other guy's dead. Theo had to shoot him."

Jameson's attention went to Theo then, and he stepped back when Jodi came out of the room and into the hall. She didn't hurry to Theo. She didn't curse him, either. Considering that he hadn't contacted her in a while, he deserved the cursing.

Ivy didn't linger in the hall, though. She pushed past all of them and hurried into the room, no doubt to see her son.

"You came because of these gunmen?" Jodi asked him.

"Yeah," Theo verified. "I tried to stop this."

Jodi made a sound of understanding, and this time she went to him. Just as he'd done to Ivy, Jodi hugged him. For a couple of seconds, anyway. But then she eased back and punched him in the arm.

Hard.

"That's for not calling me." She punched him again. "That's for letting me think you might be dead or dying somewhere."

The emotion surprised him. So did the tears that sprang to his sister's eyes. Jodi wasn't the crying sort. Or at least she hadn't been the last time he'd seen her. But she hadn't been engaged to Gabriel Beckett then. Obviously, his sister had taken her life in a new direction.

"I love you," Jodi added. "And you're bleeding." She used the sleeve of her shirt to wipe his cheek.

Theo hadn't forgotten about the glass cutting him, but he also hadn't figured it was serious since he wasn't hurting.

"Who's with Gabriel?" Jodi asked.

"Three ranch hands."

Jodi glanced back at Jameson, and that seemed to be the only cue the Ranger needed to get moving. Maybe Jodi wanted her soon-to-be husband to have as much backup as possible.

"Wait here with them," Jameson said to Theo as he headed down the stairs. "And don't let them go outside until I say so."

Theo doubted Ivy would want to venture out of the house as long as that gunman was out there, but since his sister was already nibbling on her bottom lip and looking around, she might try to disobey Jameson's orders. Just in case that's what she had on her mind, Theo took Jodi by the arm.

"Is there a bathroom in here so you can get me a cloth for this cut on my cheek?" he asked. Not that he particularly wanted to do that, but it would give Jodi something to do.

"Yes, this way."

Theo followed her into the bedroom and then to the attached bathroom. It wasn't that big, but it still took Theo a moment to spot Ivy because she was in the corner next to a clawfoot tub. She had a boy clutched in her arms.

Definitely not a baby.

This kid was older, school-age, and he was looking up at Ivy as if to comfort her rather than vice versa.

Jodi froze, practically in midstep. Ivy froze, too, but the boy turned and faced Theo. And Theo felt as if he'd just been punched in the gut. Because he knew that face. Or rather he knew the features, because he saw them every time he looked in the mirror.

Hell.

Ivy must have seen his reaction then, because she shook her head. Not a denial, exactly, since there was no way she could deny what Theo had just realized.

He was looking at his own son.

Chapter Four

Ivy could have sworn her heart stopped beating for a few seconds. Theo knew. God, he knew.

From the moment she'd seen Theo by the side of the house, Ivy had feared this might come. In fact, at first that's why she had thought Theo was there, that he'd found out about Nathan. It would have been safer if that's why he'd been there. But it wasn't going to be easy to deal with the storm that was brewing behind Theo's narrowed eyes.

"Who is that?" Nathan asked, his attention suddenly fixed on Theo. "He's not one of the bad men, is he?"

On the surface those were easy questions, but neither Ivy, Jodi nor Theo jumped to provide him with answers. Ivy wasn't even sure she could speak yet, and she doubted Theo could, either, because his jaw was clenched so tight.

"Uh, this is my brother, Theo." Jodi finally spoke up. "And no, he's not a bad guy. He's sort of a cop like your uncle Gabriel and uncle Jameson."

Because Ivy still had her arms wrapped around Nathan, she felt his muscles relax a little. It would probably be a while before he completely relaxed. Even when he did, this had changed everything for him. Her little boy had heard those gunshots, had felt the terror that went along with him.

There'd be nightmares.

Ones similar to hers, ones she'd been having for a decade. And Ivy silently cursed the gunmen for that. Silently thanked Theo, too, for warning them, or those two thugs might have made it all the way into the house. Then her son might have to deal with more than fear, tight muscles and nightmares. They could all be dead.

A thought that sickened her to the core.

At the moment, though, Theo probably wouldn't want her thanks. For anything. In fact, his shock had morphed into a glare that he was now aiming at her.

"How old are you?" Theo asked. His glare softened significantly when he looked at Nathan.

"Nine," her son answered, meaning Theo could narrow down the date he'd been conceived.

Theo clearly wasn't surprised by her son's answer. Not after seeing Nathan's face. In fact, Theo might even be able to remember the exact date of Nathan's conception. Because it was the same night of the big blowup between her parents and him. A blowup that'd happened because her mom had found Nathan and her in bed together.

All of those feelings came back, too.

Ivy pushed them aside, that mix of pleasure and grief, and she got to her feet. It was obvious there were some things she needed to say to Theo. Obvious, too, that he had some questions for her, and she didn't want him asking those in front of Nathan. Eventually, her son would have to know the truth, but now wasn't the time. He wasn't ready for it. Heck, *she* wasn't ready for it.

"I'll stay with Nathan," Jodi volunteered. "He'll be okay."

Even though Ivy hadn't said anything to

her, Jodi and she were on the same page about what needed to be done. But Ivy didn't want her explanation to Theo to come at the expense of her son's safety.

Theo didn't say anything, either. He just followed Ivy out of the ensuite bathroom and into the bedroom, and he pulled the bathroom door shut behind them. She didn't go far, just a few feet away. Hopefully close enough so she could still get to Nathan if there was another attack but far enough away from Theo so that they weren't in each other's personal space. Even though it did seem a little late for that since they'd once been lovers.

He stood there staring, and she could see he was trying to work out what to say to her. Hopefully, he wasn't going to yell at her, since she didn't want Nathan to overhear something like that. At least at the moment Theo wasn't yelling. In fact, he wasn't saying anything. Theo put his hands on his hips, shook his head and turned that glare on her again.

"Why?" he finally asked, and he did keep his voice at a whisper. An angry one that dripped with emotion.

Since that simple word could encompass a lot of territory, Ivy went with a simple explanation. "I couldn't find you to tell you I was pregnant."

Ivy watched him process that, and she knew it wasn't something he could dispute. Theo had vanished shortly after the attacks. Jodi had been in the hospital, still recovering from her horrific injuries, and she certainly hadn't known how to get in touch with her brother.

"I left because you told me to leave," Theo reminded her.

She couldn't dispute that, either. Ivy had indeed ordered him out of her house and her life after the argument with her parents. In part, she'd done that for Theo's own safety. Because she'd been afraid her father was going to beat him up or have him arrested for something. No way would Theo believe that now, though. And even if he did, it would only make him madder than he already was. He wouldn't have wanted her fighting those kind of battles for him.

"Does Nathan know the truth?" Theo snapped.

Ivy shook her head, and she prayed Theo didn't rush out and tell him.

"How about your late husband?" Theo again. "Did he know?"

"Yes. His name was Chad Vogel, and Nathan was eleven months old when I married him. But Jameson, Lauren and Gabriel didn't know I was pregnant or that I had a child. Neither did Jodi. At least they didn't know until I came back to Blue River two days ago."

Now Theo cursed. "One of them should have called me. And don't say they couldn't find me, because Jameson's a Texas Ranger. He could have tracked me down if you'd asked him to do that."

"Yes," she repeated. "And FYI, Jodi said I should tell you after she finally met Nathan day before yesterday. I just thought it was best if I waited until after the wedding to do that."

Judging from his still-tight expression, Theo didn't agree. And maybe he was right. Maybe she should have searched harder for him, especially after her husband passed away.

Theo glared at her a few more seconds before he finally glanced away and cursed some more. "Is Nathan healthy? Is he okay?"

It seemed petty for her to hesitate even a second to give him that info. But she knew that with each new bit, Theo would only want to know more and more. Then he would want Nathan to know who'd really fathered him.

Theo. And not Chad.

Of course, Nathan didn't have a lot of memories of Chad anyway, since he'd died after losing his battle with cancer when Nathan had been only five.

"I'm sorry," she said. It didn't seem nearly enough, but there wasn't much else she could say or do at this point.

There was a sound outside the window, a car engine, and Theo hurried to look while motioning for her to stay put. Just like that, her heart revved up again. Not that it'd gone back to normal, and that might not happen for a long time.

"It's just the ambulance," Theo told her. He stayed at the window with his gun drawn.

She was glad that it'd arrived. Now maybe the medics could save the gunman so they could find out what the heck was going on. And soon. It was probably too much to ask to find the person responsible for this attack and get him behind bars so that Gabriel and Jodi could get on with the wedding, but Ivy prayed that would happen. Her brother and Jodi deserved to have their special day.

"Did you love him?" Theo asked.

The sound of his voice cut through her thoughts, and it took Ivy a moment to realize that he probably wasn't talking about Nathan.

Of course she loved him. But Theo knew that and was asking about Chad.

"Yes. I did."

In some ways that was a lie, but Ivy wasn't about to get into that now. Besides, what Theo probably wanted to know was how she could go so quickly from him to another man. Especially when she'd had Theo's child. But it was because of Nathan that she'd agreed to marry Chad. Once Theo got past the initial kick of anger, she'd maybe tell him more.

More that he wasn't going to want to hear.

"Does it look as if the gunman is still alive?" Ivy said. It was definitely time for a change of subject, because whatever was going on outside that window was critical to their situation. A situation that didn't necessarily have to include Theo.

He nodded. "The guy's moving, clutching his chest."

Probably because he was bleeding and in pain. She wasn't certain of the details of his injury, but Ivy had heard Gabriel's quick phone chat that he'd had with Jameson.

And now she moved on to the part about Theo not having to be in Nathan's or her life. "For the record, I don't expect anything from you," Ivy continued a moment later. "We were practically kids when I got pregnant, and the feelings you once had for me are obviously long gone."

Theo gave her a look that could have frozen the hottest levels of Hades. "I'm not leaving," he spat out. He stared at her as if he might repeat it, but then he shook his head. "I just need to stop whoever sent those thugs, and then I can deal with everything else."

That sounded like some kind of threat. And Ivy wasn't immune to it. She'd never had to share her son with anyone. Not even Chad, who had been a "father" in name only, had been able to spend much time in the parent roll because of his health problems. She didn't feel ready to share Nathan with Theo, either.

"Yeah, we were kids," Theo went on, "but we sure as hell aren't kids now." He paused again, those jaw muscles stirring like crazy. "You should have found a way to tell me."

Ivy huffed. "You can say that now," she argued. "But we were in a different mind-set back then. Remember?"

"Of course I remember. Your mom caught us in bed. Your dad blew a fuse when she told him, and he ordered me to stay away from you. That should have been the time you backed me up, but you didn't. You agreed with him and told me to get out of the house."

Ivy had indeed told Theo to leave, but she darn sure hadn't agreed with her father. Sherman Beckett could be a hard man sometimes, and he hadn't approved of Theo and his minor run-ins with the law. Ironically, her dad had thought Theo would get her pregnant and then run out on her. Strange how all of that had worked out. Strange, too, that Theo had become a lawman, the last thing her father or she would have expected him to become.

"Then you and your brothers actually considered me a suspect in your parents' murders," Theo added. Judging from his tone, that was still an extremely sore spot for him.

It was for her, too.

Because she hadn't stuck up for Theo. That had obviously been the straw that had broken the camel's back. As soon as Theo's name had been cleared, he'd left Blue River.

Ivy was about to put an end to this conversation, or a temporary end at least, but she heard the footsteps in the hall. Both Theo and she pivoted in that direction, and she felt herself gear up for another fight. If a gunman had actually made it into the house, he wasn't getting to Nathan.

"It's me," Jameson called out.

The relief came, but it didn't completely wash away the adrenaline punch she'd gotten when she thought they could be near another attack. A moment later, the door opened, and her brother came in.

Jameson's attention went to her first, and he no doubt saw her tense body. Perhaps saw a whole lot more than that, though, when his gaze shifted to Theo. Then to the bathroom door where he knew Jodi—and Nathan—were waiting. It didn't take Jameson long to piece everything together, and he cursed under his breath.

"Just in case there's a bug in the house, I'll whisper," Jameson said. "How much trouble is this situation with Nathan going to cause the two of you?" he asked. He didn't specifically direct the question to either of them, and neither of them answered.

However, Theo did ask a question of his own, and it was indeed meant for Jameson because he was staring at her brother. "Did the gunman say anything about who sent him and why?" He, too, kept his voice at a whisper.

Ivy figured that he hadn't, but Jameson nodded. He took a deep breath, and that's when she knew this was not going to be good news.

"The gunman died right after the medics put him in the ambulance," Jameson said.

Now Ivy wanted to curse. She didn't. Over the years, motherhood had taught her to rein in the profanity, but still this was a situation that warranted some cursing.

"He didn't know who hired him," Jameson went on. "Or at least that's what he said. According to him, it was all done through a third party. A San Antonio thug everyone just called Mack. I've never heard of him, and I know most of the CIs and other informants in the area. And yeah, I've already made a call about him."

That didn't sound very promising, especially since it wasn't a name her brother knew, but Ivy got the sinking feeling that it wasn't his not knowing Mack that'd put that troubled look on his face.

"The gunman said something else," Jameson continued a moment later. "This Mack hired other men. At least three more." He turned to his sister then. "And, Ivy, they have orders to use whatever means necessary to kill *you*."

Chapter Five

"Ivy's the target?" Theo immediately asked Jameson. He figured it was a question that Ivy wanted answered, as well.

Jameson lifted his shoulder. "That's what the guy said." Like the rest of them, he continued to keep his voice at a whisper. "That doesn't mesh with what the CI told you, though, does it?"

Theo had to shake his head. "But maybe the person behind this changed his mind and decided to go after one of us at a time. He or she might think Ivy would be the easiest to pick off."

Ivy made a soft gasping sound, and Theo wished he hadn't voiced that aloud. Still, it was true. Since they didn't know the person's identity or motive, anything was possible.

"Are you okay?" Jameson asked his sister. He gave her arm a soft pat.

She shook her head as if pulling herself out of a trance. "Yes." Ivy fluttered her fingers toward the bathroom. "I just need to check on Nathan."

"Give yourself a couple of minutes," Jameson advised her. "You're as pale as paper right now, and Nathan will pick up on that."

The kid probably would. Then again, Nathan and Jodi both had to be on edge waiting for news.

"Are you okay?" Jameson repeated. Not directed at Ivy this time, but at Theo.

Theo lied with a nod. He was far from okay. His mind was whirling. Hell. He'd thought this would be a quick in-and-out trip back to the Beckett ranch, but there was no way that was possible now.

He had a son.

And if that wasn't enough to get him to stay, someone wanted Ivy dead. Of course, the gunman could have been lying when he'd said that Ivy was the target of would-be assassins, but the attack had been real. Bullets had actually been shot into the house, and even if she was the sole target, that didn't mean others couldn't have been caught in cross fire. Nathan and anyone else could have been killed.

"Look, I know you two have plenty to work out," Jameson went on, "but you need to leave it here for now. Gabriel wants to take everyone to the sheriff's office. The medics will need to take a look at that, too."

It took Theo a moment to realize Jameson meant the cut on Theo's cheek. "I don't want a medic," Theo insisted. "But someone should check on Jodi and Nathan."

It wasn't the first time he'd said his son's name aloud, but for some reason, it hit him like a punch to the gut. Theo actually had to take a moment just to regather his breath.

"Yeah," Jameson mumbled. Whatever the heck that meant. "You both stay here, pull yourselves together, and I'll go in and talk to Nathan and Jodi. Be ready to leave as soon as Gabriel has the cruisers in place."

Jameson stepped into the bathroom, shutting the door and leaving Ivy and him alone. Since Theo didn't want to keep glaring at her, he turned his attention back to the window so he could watch for the cruisers.

"Why would Gabriel want us to go to the sheriff's office?" she asked, her voice shaky.

"Wouldn't it be safer to stay here rather than risk going outside?"

"No. There could be other gunmen in the area. Plus, he probably wants to set up some security measures here." He glanced at her and saw that didn't do anything to ease the tension on her face. "Gabriel knows what he's doing."

Theo hoped that was true, anyway. There was no love lost between Gabriel and him, but Ivy's brother had been sheriff for nearly a decade now. Maybe that meant he knew how to handle an attempted murder investigation along with keeping Ivy and the others safe. Theo had no intentions, though, of just backing off and letting Gabriel run with this. Not when his son's safety was at stake.

"When I first saw Nathan, he asked who I was," Theo reminded her. "He thinks your late husband is his dad?"

She paused a long time, and it was so quiet that Theo could hear Jameson talking in the bathroom. He couldn't hear what the Ranger was saying. Which was a good thing. Because it meant Nathan wouldn't be able to hear what Theo and Ivy were talking about.

"No. Nathan knows the truth," Ivy finally answered. "Chad was a widower and a lot older than me. He had a college-age daughter, Lacey, when we got married. Lacey told Nathan when he was about six." Her mouth tightened enough to let him know that was a sore subject. "My stepdaughter and I don't get along that well," she added.

Theo made a mental note of the woman's name. Right now, he needed to look at all the angles to figure out who was behind this, and a riled stepdaughter could definitely have motive for putting this together.

Of course, so could Uncle August.

Theo would be contacting him very, very soon.

August had been a thorn in nearly everyone's side since his brother's arrest for the Beckett murders. For whatever reason, August had become Travis's champion of so-called justice even though Travis had never asked him to do that. In fact, from everything Theo had heard, his father had accepted his fate and was willing to spend the rest of his life behind bars.

His phone buzzed, and Theo answered it when he saw Wesley's name on the screen. "I heard about the shooting at the ranch," Wesley greeted. "I'm still in Blue River, so you want me to head out there?"

"No need. The danger seems to be contained. For now, anyway." Theo didn't mention they'd all soon be going to the sheriff's office since this wasn't a whispered phone conversation. If there truly was a bug in the house, he didn't want to tip off the gunmen's boss about them leaving, since that would mean they'd be out in the open, at least for a little while.

"The deputy here got an update from Gabriel," Wesley went on. "The gunmen didn't ID the person who hired them."

"No. But I've got a lead. I'll tell you about it when I see you."

"A lead?" Wesley practically snapped. "Who?"

"The house might be bugged," Theo reminded him. "The info I got might not amount to anything, but it's a start."

"Text me what you have," Wesley added a moment later.

Theo hadn't thought it possible, but Wesley seemed even more on edge than Theo did. "I will." Theo ended the call so he could do that, but the bathroom door opened before he could even get started on the text.

And Nathan came out.

Jameson was in front of him. Jodi, behind.

Both still had their guns in hand. Nathan gave Theo a long look, and Theo wondered if the boy recognized their similar features. If so, he didn't say anything. He just hurried to his mom, and Ivy looped her arms around him, pulling him close to her.

"Gabriel wants us in the cruisers," Jameson mouthed to Ivy and him. "Don't take anything with you in case it's bugged."

It was a good precaution, and while Theo wasn't exactly eager to have Ivy or Nathan outside, he understood why they were in a hurry when they followed Jameson out of the room and to the stairs. There wasn't exactly a peaceful, safe feeling in the house right now.

Jodi paused long enough for their gazes to connect, and he saw the questions in her eyes. How was he handling this? It was too long of an answer and one that he couldn't give her with just a mere glance.

When they made it to the front of the house, Theo spotted the two cruisers that were now parked by the porch steps. There was a deputy behind the wheel of one of them and another deputy next to him, but Gabriel was driving the cruiser in front. "Ride with me so we can talk," Gabriel insisted. He motioned for them to get in with him, and he threw open both the back door and the passenger's side.

"Hurry," Jameson reminded them. "Jodi and I will ride in front. Theo, Ivy and Nathan in the back seat."

Jameson didn't have to tell them twice to hurry. Jodi and he took off running, and Theo got Ivy and Nathan moving fast. Nathan ended up in the middle between Ivy and him, and the moment they were buckled up, Gabriel got them out of there. The deputies followed right behind them, no doubt as backup in case there was another attack.

"Is everyone okay?" Gabriel asked.

Gabriel brushed a kiss on Jodi's forehead, and when his sister looked at her soon-to-be husband, Theo could practically see the love in her eyes. Not really a surprise, though. He had always suspected that Jodi was in love with Gabriel, and despite their painful pasts, it appeared that Gabriel felt the same way about her.

Each of them, including Theo, answered or made some kind of sound to indicate they were okay.

"He's not all right," Nathan said, and he motioned toward Theo. "He's bleeding."

Theo didn't exactly thank him for pointing that out, because Nathan seemed to be alarmed by the blood. Theo hated to add to the boy's anxiety, but he also didn't want anyone to make a fuss about a small cut. At least he thought it was small. He hadn't really had a chance to look at it, but he did know that his cheek was stinging.

Jameson opened the glove compartment, located a small first-aid kit and passed it not to Theo but to Ivy. "Since Theo said he won't see a medic, you make sure he doesn't need stitches."

That request seemed to add to Ivy's anxiety level, but she opened the kit and took out some gauze and antiseptic cream. She reached over Nathan and blotted the gauze against Theo's cut. It wasn't a very manly reaction, but he grunted from the pain.

"When Mom's fixing up my cuts," Nathan said, "I just think about a computer game or my horse, Willow. You have a horse?" he asked Theo.

Theo shook his head, but nearly cursed when that caused Ivy to press harder on his cheek. He decided it was best to keep still. Best not to make direct eye contact with Nathan, either, since it was obvious the boy was curious about him. Soon, Theo would satisfy that curiosity by telling him the truth, that he was his father. But for now, Theo just let Ivy continue to torture him while he kept watch around them.

Other than the cruiser behind them, there were no other vehicles in sight. Theo wanted to keep it like that. If he'd been alone, however, he would have wanted this SOB to come after him. That way, he could stop him and put an end to this.

No one in the car talked about the attack, though Theo was certain they wanted to do that. Best to wait until Nathan was out of earshot. The boy had already witnessed enough without having the details spelled out for him.

Two men dead.

Countless shots fired.

And a threat still hanging over their heads because this snake might indeed go after Ivy.

Once Ivy was finished cleaning and bandaging the cut, Theo took out his phone and texted a fellow DEA agent in the San Antonio office so they could get started on locating this thug named Mack. He didn't include Wesley on this, but he would fill him in at the sheriff's office. As soon as Theo was certain there were no bugs in the place. It was bad enough that he had Jodi, Nathan and Ivy on the road, but he didn't want anyone else knowing they were on their way to Gabriel's office.

It wasn't that far from the ranch to town, and Gabriel didn't dawdle. He made it there in probably record time, and he pulled the cruiser to a stop at the back door so they could hurry inside. First through the break room and then into Gabriel's office. Even though it was a good twenty feet away from the squad room at the front of the building, Wesley must have heard them, because he came hurrying back.

Ivy automatically stopped, and she pulled Nathan behind her. Jodi rushed to Ivy's side to shield the boy, as well. Jameson and Gabriel reacted, too, by taking aim at the man.

"This is DEA agent Wesley Sanford," Theo explained. "He's the one who gave me the recording from the CI."

That caused Gabriel and Jameson to relax a bit, but Jodi and Ivy still stayed in a defensive posture. Maybe because Wesley didn't exactly have a welcoming expression. Probably because he'd been in law enforcement most of his adult life, first as a San Antonio cop and then as a DEA agent. The man was tall and lanky with a thin face, and he rarely smiled. He certainly wasn't smiling now.

"You said you had a lead," Wesley reminded him, "and that you'd text me."

"*Possible* lead," Theo corrected. He motioned toward Gabriel. "This is Sheriff Beckett and his brother, Ranger Jameson Beckett. Are you certain the building isn't bugged?" he added to Wesley.

"The deputies and I have gone through the place and didn't see anything."

"I'm having the Rangers bring in equipment to check every inch," Jameson volunteered. "They should be here any minute. Until then, anything we say should be in one of the interrogation rooms."

Good idea. There was minimal furniture, and a person wouldn't have had easy access to those rooms to plant a listening device. Normally, the other option would have been to discuss this outside, but there was nothing normal about this situation.

Nathan was a reminder of that.

"Why don't you stay with Nathan here in Gabriel's office?" Theo suggested to Ivy.

She instantly looked torn, and Theo knew why. Ivy wanted to hear anything about the investigation, but she didn't want their son to be part of it. Neither did Theo. Jodi must have picked up on their wanting to protect

Nathan, because she slipped her arm around the boy's shoulders and led him deeper into Gabriel's office.

"I'll wait in here with Nathan," Jodi offered. "I can probably download a movie or book for him."

"Is everything gonna be okay?" Nathan asked, volleying glances at his mom, his uncles and Theo.

"Of course," Ivy jumped in to say. Jodi, Gabriel and Jameson answered similarly.

Nathan settled his attention on Theo. Maybe because he didn't respond to the boy's question. "Will it be okay?" Nathan pressed.

Theo wasn't sure why Nathan wanted to hear his assurance when they'd only met a short while earlier. Maybe Nathan felt the connection? But Theo knew that could be wishful thinking on his part. He certainly felt a connection to his son, and it didn't matter that he hadn't shared the same years with the boy that Ivy had.

"We're all going to work to put a stop to this," Theo finally told him.

Nathan nodded, apparently accepting that as gospel, and he went with Jodi when she led him to Gabriel's desk. Part of Theo wanted to stay so he could just talk to him and get to know him better, but as long as Ivy was in danger, so was Nathan.

Gabriel motioned for them to follow him to one of the interview rooms just up the hall, and once they were inside, Gabriel shut the door. Each of them re-holstered their weapons. Except for Ivy. No holster for her, so she tucked the gun in the back waistband of her jeans.

"One of the gunmen gave us a first name or possibly a nickname of the person who hired him," Theo told Wesley. "Mack, someone the gunman described as a thug from San Antonio. Ring any bells?"

Wesley repeated the name, and he nodded. "Maybe. There's a bar. A *seedy* bar," Wesley added. "It's owned by a guy whose last name is McKenzie. I can't remember his first name, but he used to work as a bouncer at the place before he bought it." He took out his phone, stepping slightly away from them. "I'll see what I can find."

"I need to check on my own contacts," Jameson said, taking out his phone, as well. "I also need to keep tabs on anything the ME might find on our dead guys. Anything the CSIs might find, too."

Yes, because those gunmen had gotten to

the ranch somehow, and that meant they'd maybe left a vehicle in the area. A vehicle that could contain possible clues as to who had hired them and why.

"I'll get to work on ID'ing the guys," Gabriel said. "Once we have that, then we might be able to find a money trail."

Again, it was a good idea, and Gabriel moved as if he might step to the other side of the room to start on that, but he stopped and looked at his sister. Then at Theo. "I don't want any yelling," Gabriel warned Theo.

That didn't sit right with Theo. Of course, nothing much would at this point unless they found the clown who'd orchestrated all of this. But Gabriel wasn't talking about the danger. He was talking about Nathan.

"You don't think I have a right to yell?" Theo asked him.

Gabriel's eyes narrowed for just a moment. "Maybe. But it won't happen here. Anything you and my sister have to hash out can wait."

With that "advice" doled out, Gabriel moved away from them and made a call. Of course, that left Ivy and Theo standing there, staring at each other. Theo knew he had his own calls to make. And he wanted to check on this situation with Ivy's stepdaughter to make sure she didn't hate Ivy enough to do something like that. And Theo did pull his phone from his pocket, but Ivy spoke before he could make a call.

"Don't tell Nathan that you're his father," she said. "Let me do it, please."

Theo thought about that for a few moments. "What will you say to him?"

"The truth. More or less," she added. "I don't want to get into specifics. I'll just tell him that it didn't work out between us."

He gave that more thought, too. "I don't want him to think I knew about him and then left. I'm not the bad guy in all of this."

Something flashed through her eyes. Not anger. But hurt. Theo wished he'd phrased that better, but it was the truth. There was only one person who knew Ivy was carrying Theo's child, and that was Ivy herself.

Ivy nodded, finally. "I'll tell him I screwed up," she said, dodging his gaze. But she didn't do the dodging before he saw something else in her eyes.

Tears.

Hell. It was too bad Gabriel hadn't added "no crying" along with the "no yelling." Theo wasn't an ice man—not every day, anyway— and those tears cut away at him. They also brought memories back to the surface. Ivy had been crying the night she'd ended things with him. He hadn't wanted to hold her and comfort her then. Too much anger had been bubbling up inside him. But for some stupid reason he wanted to try to comfort her now.

He resisted.

In part because it truly would be stupid to have her back in his arms and also because her brothers were watching her. Jameson and Gabriel were both on their phones, but they had their attention nailed to their kid sister.

Gabriel finished his call first and came back to them, and judging from his expression he looked ready to blast Theo for making Ivy cry. But Ivy gave a little shake of her head, a gesture for her brother to back off. Gabriel did—eventually.

"They got an immediate match on one of the gunmen's prints," Gabriel explained several long moments later. "Ted Mintor. He has a long record, and they're looking for a match on the second one."

Good. A name could lead them to possible bank records. From what Theo could hear of Jameson's conversation, he was already working on that.

"I'm having the hands beef up security at

the ranch," Gabriel went on. He was looking at his sister now. "I'm debating whether to go back there or move Nathan, Jodi and you to a safe house."

"Jodi won't go," Theo quickly said.

Gabriel didn't argue with that. Probably because he knew Jodi well. Jodi was a well-trained security specialist and would consider it an insult if she was tucked away while others were in danger. But maybe Theo could put a different spin on this to get her to go.

"What if Jodi realizes she'd be protecting Ivy and Nathan if she went?" Theo asked.

Gabriel nodded. "That could work. It'd also work if you went with them. That way, I wouldn't have to tie up a deputy."

Theo felt as if Gabriel had just turned the tables on him. He did want to be with Ivy and Nathan. He wanted to protect them. But it would be hard to find the person behind this if he was shut away in a safe house.

Before Theo could respond to Gabriel, Wesley finished his call and joined them. Theo could tell from the agent's expression that he'd learned something.

Something that Theo might not like.

"I just had a tech do a computer search on our person of interest," Wesley explained.

"Birch McKenzie. Like I said, he owns a bar in San Antonio, and it's not exactly a five-star place. When I was a beat cop, we were always getting calls to go out to the place. Anyway, SAPD's bringing in McKenzie now for questioning, but the tech found an interesting connection. To you," he added, looking at Theo.

Theo shook his head and was certain he'd never heard the man's name before today. "You think I know McKenzie?"

"No. But your uncle August does." Wesley paused, his mouth tightening. "August lent McKenzie the money to buy the bar."

Gabriel mumbled some profanity under his breath and took out his phone again. "I'll get August in here right away for questioning. And he'd better have the right answers."

Chapter Six

Ivy tried to put on a brave face for her son's sake, but she felt none of that braveness inside her. She was terrified, not for herself but for Nathan. He was much too young to be caught up in the middle of this.

"How much longer do we have to be here?" Nathan asked her. Considering they'd been at Gabriel's office for well over an hour, she was surprised he hadn't asked that sooner. Maybe, though, that was because he'd been interested in the movie Jodi had downloaded for him.

"We'll be able to leave soon," Ivy told him, and hoped it wasn't a lie. Actually, she wasn't certain how long it would take Gabriel to set up a safe house.

One where Nathan, Jodi and she would apparently be going. With Theo. That caused her stomach to tighten even more than it already was. Because there was little chance that Theo would keep the truth from Nathan much longer.

"But what about Aunt Jodi and Uncle Gabriel's wedding?" Nathan pressed. He yawned. No surprise there, since it was a little past his nine o'clock bedtime. Plus, it'd been the day from Hades what with the attack.

"We might have to delay that a day or two," Jodi answered. She was in the corner of Gabriel's office, working on a laptop. Theo was in the other corner, doing the same. All of them waiting for the deputy to bring in August.

Nathan made a sound of disappointment. In his case it was probably because he'd been expecting cake and party food. But Ivy figured what he felt was a drop in the bucket compared to what Jodi and Gabriel did. They'd waited a long time for this wedding, and now it might have to be delayed indefinitely.

Jodi stood, stretching, and she set the laptop aside. "I'm getting a bottle of water. Anyone else want one?"

Theo, Nathan and Ivy shook their heads. Gabriel had already brought in burgers from the café just up the street, and the only one who'd touched any of it was Nathan. Nothing seemed to dampen his appetite.

Jodi stepped out, closing the door behind her. A precaution no doubt, so that Nathan wouldn't be able to hear anything that was being said in the squad room where Gabriel, Jameson, Wesley and two deputies were working.

"It's like there are a bunch of secrets going on," Nathan said, snagging both Ivy's and Theo's attention. Nathan looked at both of them, probably waiting for them to verify that.

They didn't.

Mumbling something she didn't catch, her son got up from the desk and went to the small bed that Ivy had made for him on the floor. Basically, it was a couple of blankets and a pillow that she'd gotten from the break room. It wouldn't be long before Nathan was sacked out—which was a good thing, considering the loud voice she heard out in the squad room.

Not August Canton.

But it was a familiar voice.

"Lacey," Ivy provided when Theo looked at her.

Ivy got up, and with Theo in front of her, they stepped into the hall. Yes, it was her stepdaughter all right, though it was hard for

Ivy to think of Lacey as any kind of daughter since they were practically the same age.

"You did this," Lacey snapped the moment her attention landed on Ivy.

Ivy first checked on Nathan. He was indeed going to sleep, so once Jodi was back in the office with him, Ivy pulled the door shut so this wouldn't disturb him. The trick, though, would be to keep Lacey's voice in the normal range. She looked ready to start yelling.

Gabriel stepped in front of Lacey, but she just tried to go around him. "I want to have a little chat with Mommie Dearest. Because of her, the cops want to talk to me."

"And *I* want to talk to you," Theo snarled right back, and there was no shred of friendliness in his tone.

Lacey peered around Gabriel, and the moment she actually looked at Theo, her eyes widened a little. She didn't smile exactly, but it was close.

"Theo Canton," Lacey provided.

Because Theo's arm was against Ivy's, she felt him tense a little. "How do you know me?"

"I've made it my business to know you and anyone else associated with my dad's wife. Your name and picture were in the papers.

You were a suspect in the murders of Ivy's parents." The slight smile stayed on her face.

And Ivy knew why. Even though she'd never told Lacey about Nathan's father, Lacey could no doubt see the resemblance. Of course, the papers that'd covered the murders had gone into the fact that Theo and Ivy had broken up that night and that was his possible motive for murder. It wouldn't be a stretch for Lacey to do the math and realize that Nathan had been born nine months later.

"So," Lacey said, dragging that out a few syllables. Her attention stayed fixed to Theo. "What'd you want to see me about?"

He went closer. "Someone tried to kill us. What do you know about that?"

Despite Theo's harsh tone, Lacey hardly reacted. Instead, she turned to Ivy. "You put him up to this. You want him to suspect me of something I didn't do so you can get me out of the way. Well, it won't work. I'm not stopping the fight to get what's rightfully mine."

Ivy groaned softly. "Chad left everything to Nathan and me in his will," she explained to Theo.

"Because you brainwashed him," Lacey insisted. "I've filed a lawsuit to rescind his will and give me what's rightfully mine."

"Your father didn't want you to have that money," Ivy reminded her. This was old news to Lacey, but Ivy repeated it, anyway. "He thought you already had too much from your mother's trust fund and that you needed to learn some responsibility."

Lacey cursed. "You don't know me, and you don't have a right to say anything like that to me. He was my dad."

"And he was my husband," Ivy pointed out just as quickly.

"Are you here for your interrogation?" Gabriel asked when Lacey opened her mouth, no doubt to return verbal fire.

Lacey gave him a withering look. "By you? I think not. You're Ivy's brother. And not you, either," she added to Theo. "I won't have Ivy's ex-boyfriend trying to pin something on me."

"What about me?" Wesley asked, standing. "I'm not related to Ivy or Theo. And the sooner you answer questions, the sooner we can clear your name. Or maybe you'd rather I take you into custody now and drive you back to my San Antonio office."

Maybe in that moment it occurred to Lacey that it hadn't been a good idea to come storming into a sheriff's office with wild accusations against the sheriff's sister. She was almost certainly weighing her options, and considering her expression, she didn't like any of them.

"I'm not talking to anyone unless my lawyer is here," Lacey concluded.

"Then you'd best be calling him or her right now," Gabriel said, and he added a glare to it.

Lacey glared back. Cursed. But she took out her phone to make the call to her attorney.

"Get her into the other interview room," Gabriel told Wesley and Jameson. "She can wait for her lawyer there."

When Gabriel looked out the window, Ivy followed his gaze and realized why there'd been some urgency in her brother's order. That's because August had just gotten out of his car and was making a beeline for the sheriff's office.

Round two was about to hit.

Wesley and Jameson had barely enough time to get Lacey out of there before August came waltzing in. Ivy braced herself for August to unleash some anger on Theo. After all, August had always said that Jodi and Theo hadn't done nearly enough to help clear their father's name. But unlike Lacey, there was no anger on August's face or in his body language.

"Ivy," August greeted. "Welcome home. It's been a long time."

Yes, it had been. Ten years. She would never be able to make her brothers understand why she'd cut them out of her life. Sometimes, she didn't understand it, either.

August was the same as he had been ten years ago, and he still didn't look as if he ran his brother's ranch. He dressed more like a rich businessman, emphasis on the rich. And he was. In fact, he probably had as much money or more than Ivy's family thanks to August's wealthy mother, who'd died shortly after marrying Travis's father and giving birth to August. Travis, on the other hand, had been a cowboy. One with a drinking problem. And despite the fact that August and Travis had been as different as night and day, that hadn't stopped August from spearheading the fight to clear Travis's name.

August turned to Theo next, and while Ivy wasn't sure how the man would react, she certainly hadn't expected him to go to Theo and hug him. Clearly, Theo hadn't expected it, either, because she saw him go stiff.

"Good to have you home, Theo," August said.

Ivy was instantly suspicious. August had always been somewhat of a hothead, and from everything Ivy had heard from Jodi, August had plenty of resentment for Theo.

"Will you be seeing your dad?" August asked when he stepped back from that hug.

"No," Theo said without hesitation.

Now there was that flash of anger in August's eyes that she'd been expecting. He aimed some of that anger at her. "Then why are you here?" August didn't wait for him to answer. "Oh, I get it. You came for Jodi's wedding. That figures. Instead of her saying 'I do,' you two should be helping me. Did you know your dad has been stuck in prison all this time?"

Ivy knew that, of course, but it caused her breath to go thin just thinking about it. She wanted Travis to pay for her parents' murders, but nothing they did now, including Travis spending the rest of his life behind bars, would bring them back.

"I know," Theo answered. "But he was convicted of murder."

More anger went through August's eyes. "On circumstantial evidence. Heck, he doesn't remember anything about that night, and that's why it was so easy for the Becketts to pin this on him."

Since there were three Becketts in the room, August obviously didn't mind letting them know he thought they had railroaded his brother. They hadn't. She started to remind him that when Travis had been found that night, he'd had her father's blood on him. But August knew that, too, and he probably thought they'd planted it there.

Or else maybe August had been the one to do the planting.

"There was another attack at the ranch," Ivy said.

August nodded. "Yeah, whenever somebody goes after you or your kin, your brothers start hauling me in for questioning. They have this warped notion that if I kill one of them, or you, then it'll get Travis out of jail. It won't. The only thing that'll do that is for the truth to come out."

Both Jameson and Gabriel huffed as if this were old news. It gave her a glimpse of what they'd been having to deal with for the past decade.

"So, is that why you told me to come?" August went on. "Because you want to pin this latest attack on me?"

"Yes," Theo readily admitted. "Did you have anything to do with it?"

August tossed him a glare before he gave one to Gabriel, Jameson and her. "No. Of course not." He turned to Theo to finish that. "Your father loves both your sister and you. Why, I don't know, since you rarely go to see him. But if I were going to do something to help him, it wouldn't be by harming one of you."

Gabriel stepped closer to August. "Then explain your connection to the man who hired the two gunmen who came after us."

No glare this time. August's eyes widened. "What the hell are you talking about?"

"Birch McKenzie," Gabriel said.

Ivy carefully watched August's reaction. First, there was more surprise, and then he cursed. "Birch didn't hire those men. Someone's setting him up, and by doing so, they're setting me up, too." He cursed again, snapped back to Theo. "I wouldn't have done this."

August was so adamant about it that Ivy almost believed him. Almost. But then she remembered that his loyalty wasn't to anyone but his brother. Why, she didn't know. Since Travis was a lot older than August, maybe he saw Travis as more of a father than a half brother. Of course, there was another reason, too.

August had had motive to kill her parents.

Like Theo and Travis, August had also had a recent run-in with Ivy's father. August hated him, and there'd been a long feud between them over land rights. Maybe August had killed them, and if so, his guilty conscience could be causing him to do everything humanly possible to free his brother from jail.

That wasn't a new theory, either. Both of her brothers had been investigating it, especially now that the threatening letters and emails had started. Someone was sending those, and it wasn't Travis since he didn't have computer access in his maximum-security cell. Also, his mail was being monitored.

While August stood there still mumbling profanity, the door to Gabriel's office opened. Both Ivy and Theo instantly looked over their shoulders to see Jodi pulling Nathan back into the room.

"Sorry," Jodi said to them. "He woke up and got to the door ahead of me."

"Mom?" Nathan rubbed his eyes and yawned. "When can we leave?"

"Soon," Ivy assured him, and Jodi took him back into the office and shut the door.

But not before August had gotten a glimpse of her son.

Just as Theo and everyone else had done,

August saw the resemblance, and he smiled. He moved as if he might go to Nathan, but both Theo and she stepped in front of him.

"So, I guess things weren't as over between you two as you thought," August said. "Are you two back together?"

"No," Theo and she said in unison. It was Theo who continued. "I came back because I got a warning about an attack at the Beckett Ranch. Ivy could be the target." He leaned in closer. "But if she's the target, then her son is in danger, too."

"Your son," August corrected.

Theo didn't confirm that. Didn't deny it, either. "If Travis really doesn't want Jodi and me hurt, then how do you think he would feel about someone harming that little boy?"

Travis's grandson. Theo didn't spell that out, but August clearly understood what Theo was saying. And his eyes narrowed again.

"What will it take to convince Jodi and you that I'm not behind the attacks?" August asked.

"Proof," Theo said. "Proof of who's doing this. And if it's not you, then I'll owe you an apology. For now, though, you have some questions to answer."

"Questions that I'll be asking in the interview room," Gabriel stated, and he motioned for August to follow him.

Thank goodness Jodi had shut the door so that August couldn't get another glimpse of Nathan. It wasn't pettiness on her part. Ivy just didn't want her son to be exposed to his great-uncle until she was certain August was indeed innocent.

Theo looked at her. The kind of look that asked if she was okay. She wasn't. Her nerves were right there at the surface, and Theo must have seen that, because he muttered some profanity under his breath.

"Why don't we go ahead and take Ivy, Nathan and Jodi to the safe house," Jameson suggested. As they'd done in the house, he kept his voice at a whisper.

"It's ready?" Ivy asked.

Jameson nodded. "Just don't expect too much. I didn't have a lot of time to put it together."

Ivy was about to say she didn't care about that, but then it hit her. "What if Nathan gets hurt because of me?" she asked. "The gunman said I was the target."

"And he could have been lying," Theo pointed out just as quickly. He huffed. "I'd rather Nathan and you not be under the same roof as our suspects."

He had a point. Of course, the real culprit could be out there, waiting for them to leave so he or she could attack again. Maybe it was someone who wasn't even on their radar. Her parents' murders had drawn a lot of press, and it was entirely possible this was a sicko who'd glommed on to them. A sicko who was not only sending threatening emails and letters, but a person who could also hire thugs to kill them.

"I'll pull the cruiser up to the back door," Jameson offered. "Once I have all of you settled, then I can come back here and help Gabriel with the interrogations."

Jameson headed off to do that, but before he made it into the hall, his phone buzzed. "SAPD," her brother said, looking at the screen.

He took the call but didn't put it on speaker. Since this could be an update on the case, Ivy decided to wait to go in and tell Jodi and Nathan about plans to leave for the safe house. She couldn't hear Jameson's conversation, but whatever the caller had said to him, it caused Jameson's forehead to bunch up.

"What?" Jameson snapped a moment later. He paused, listening. "You're sure?"

Ivy glanced at Theo to see if he knew what was going on, but he only shook his head.

"Birch McKenzie's dead," Jameson said when he finally ended the call. "Murdered. A gunshot wound to the head."

Ivy hadn't known the man, of course, but he'd been the link between the gunmen and the person who'd hired them. A link, too, to August.

"Who killed him?" Theo asked.

"SAPD doesn't know. They went out to question him about his possible involvement in this, and they found him dead. The cops also found his phone, and they glanced through his recent calls. The last call he made was to one of our suspects."

"August," Ivy muttered.

But Jameson shook his head. "No, McKenzie called Lacey."

Chapter Seven

As little sleep as Theo had managed to get, he figured Ivy had gotten even less. After they'd arrived at the safe house, she'd quickly taken Nathan to the room they would share, but since Theo's room was right next to theirs, he'd heard someone moving around in there most of the night. He figured that someone was Ivy.

He showered and made his way into the kitchen to get some coffee started, but got confirmation that Ivy hadn't slept when he saw her at the kitchen table already sipping a cup. Her eyes confirmed his theory, too. She looked exhausted.

And beautiful.

Yeah, Ivy was probably one of the few women on the planet who could have managed that. Despite her rumpled hair and tired eyes, she still looked amazing.

He felt that old ripple of attraction. Always did whenever he was around her. But he told that attraction to take a hike. It would only distract him at a time when he needed no other distractions. And besides, he still hadn't cooled off from her not telling him about Nathan.

"Are Jodi and Nathan still sleeping?" he asked.

She nodded. "But I figure they'll be up soon. Anything new on the case?" she added. "I heard you talking on the phone a couple of times."

He had, but Theo felt he'd gotten nowhere. "Gabriel questioned Lacey, and she denied knowing McKenzie. Lacey said he called her to set her up."

Ivy groaned, and Theo silently groaned with her. With his coffee in hand, he went to the window to look out. The safe house was on an old ranch, only about thirty miles from Blue River, and it was out in the middle of nowhere. Which was a good thing. The pastures were flat, and he had a clear view of the road. That meant it'd be hard for someone to sneak up on them. Added to that, Jameson had put out a motion detector on the road to alert them if anyone drove up.

"Lacey lawyered up," Theo went on. "So did August. And Gabriel doesn't have enough to hold either of them. That means we're at a stalemate unless SAPD or the CSIs find something to link the attack or McKenzie's murder to someone."

Someone in this case being August or Lacey.

And that brought Theo back to something he'd been wanting to ask Ivy. "Just how much does Lacey hate you?"

She looked at him for a moment before she answered. "A lot. Why?"

He lifted his shoulder. "Lacey said she made it a point to get to know anyone connected to you. It's a long shot, but she could have discovered the link between August and McKenzie."

He was talking softly enough not to wake Jodi and Nathan, and Ivy got up from the table to go closer to him, probably so she'd be able to hear him better.

"But if she wanted to set up August to take the blame for this," Ivy said, "then why would she have allowed McKenzie to call her?"

"Maybe she didn't allow it. He could have

just screwed up. Or it could be he got spooked when he realized someone was trying to kill him and he tried to get in touch with her. Either way, McKenzie would have been a loose end."

That was true even if Lacey or August wasn't behind this. McKenzie had a link to two dead gunmen, and the mastermind pulling their strings wouldn't have wanted to keep McKenzie around.

"August's motive is to clear Travis's name," Ivy whispered. "But Lacey won't inherit her father's money if she kills me." She made a soft gasp and touched her fingers to her mouth. "She'd have to get rid of Nathan, too."

That wiped away the fatigue in Ivy's eyes, and the fear quickly came. Theo had had a similar reaction earlier when he'd thought of how this might all play out.

"God, she can't hurt him," Ivy said on a rise of breath. Tears sprang to her eyes.

Hell. He didn't handle these tears any better than he had the ones the night before at the sheriff's office. This time, though, Theo put his arm around her.

Ivy melted against him.

That definitely wasn't good because she felt soft—and right—in his arms. The years vanished, and for a few seconds, she was his lover again. Thankfully, it didn't go past the thought stage because Ivy pulled away from him.

"Sorry," she said, her voice low. He wasn't sure if she was apologizing for the tears or the reaction they'd just had to each other. And Theo decided it was best if he didn't have the answer to that.

"I'm not going to let anything happen to Nathan," Theo promised her, and somehow that was a promise he'd keep.

She stayed at the window with him, and her gaze connected with his again. "Is there something you aren't telling me?" she asked. "You're not thinking of telling Nathan the truth, are you?"

That was two unrelated questions. "Nathan will eventually need to know," he reminded her.

She kept staring at him. "But?"

"It can wait a little while longer."

He was pretty sure the breath she blew out was one of relief. "Then what's wrong?"

"It's maybe nothing." And that's why Theo hated to even say it aloud. Still, it was bothering him. "It's about Lacey and Wesley. By any chance, did she ever mention him?"

"No." Ivy had the reaction that Theo expected. Confusion and surprise. "Why?"

"Wesley didn't even ask who Lacey was when she came into the sheriff's office. At that point, we weren't expecting her."

"Yes," she agreed after several moments. "But you don't think Wesley could be behind the attack?"

Theo certainly didn't want to believe it, but he just couldn't shake this feeling. "I've worked with Wesley a long time. In fact, we were teamed up on our last case where a fellow DEA agent was murdered."

She shook her head. "You believe the attack last night could somehow be connected to that?"

Theo scrubbed his hand over his face. "If it is, I can't see it."

That didn't mean he would stop looking, though. He would also be more careful about the info he got from Wesley. After all, it was Wesley's intel about the impending attack that had sent Theo running to the ranch.

"I called a DEA friend this morning," Theo explained. "His name is Matt Krueger, and he's someone I know I can trust. I asked him to look for any connections between Lacey and Wesley. Between Wesley and any of this," he added.

"But why would Wesley want to go after you?" she pressed. "Why would he want to go after you like this?" Ivy amended. "By including our families?"

"This is just a guess, but the attack last night could be the ultimate smoke screen, a way of making sure no suspicion fell on Wesley."

Still, that didn't answer one big question. Why?

Was it somehow connected to the botched investigation and death of the DEA agent? Theo had spent hours going over every transcript and all the surveillance footage he could get his hands on, and even though he couldn't see anything wrong, he felt it. Deep in his gut. Something about all of it wasn't right.

"Are you thinking that Wesley could be dirty?" she asked.

He had to shrug. "That whole undercover operation had hitches right from the start," Theo explained. He couldn't give her some details because they were classified, but he could tell her the big picture. "There was a militia group dealing arms and drugs, and some of those came from a cache of weapons that'd been seized in a federal raid. The agent who was killed was at the heart of both the bust to seize those weapons and the undercover operation of the militia group."

And now that the agent was dead, there was no way he could answer the questions that were eating away at Theo.

"God," she said. "If Wesley had anything to do with this…"

"Wesley doesn't know the location of the safe house," Theo told her when he realized all of this had put the alarm back in her eyes. "Only Jameson, Gabriel and the four of us know. And just in case something else goes wrong, if someone did manage to follow us, Jameson is working on setting up a second safe house. A backup."

The sound of footsteps stopped him from saying anything else, and Theo automatically slid his hand over his gun in his holster. But it wasn't a threat. It was Nathan.

"Aunt Jodi's taking a shower," he greeted. "Is there any cereal and milk? I'm hungry."

Ivy went to the counter, where there were bags of groceries and supplies, and she rummaged through them. "No cereal, but there are some granola bars."

Nathan didn't seem disappointed with that,

and he opened the fridge to take out the carton of milk. Since he couldn't reach the cabinet and because Ivy was opening the box of granola bars, Theo got a glass for him and set it on the table. Nathan poured himself a glass, all the while keeping his attention on Theo.

"I'm not dumb, you know," Nathan said. "I heard Aunt Jodi and Uncle Gabriel on the phone. She was whispering, but I heard her." He had a big drink of the milk. "You're my dad, aren't you?"

Even though Theo could feel the question coming, it was still a shock to hear it. A shock for Ivy, too, because she stood there, her hand frozen while she reached out to give Nathan the granola bar.

"Yeah, I am," Theo answered. He braced himself in case Ivy was going to blast him for revealing that, but she merely put the bar on the table and sank down in the chair next to Nathan.

Nathan nodded. "We look alike. Aunt Jodi said."

His sister was a regular font of information, but Theo couldn't fault her for that. Nathan was her nephew, and with Ivy keeping that a secret, it meant she'd kept Nathan a secret from all of them.

"We do look alike," Theo agreed, and he turned to Ivy to see if she had anything to add to that.

"Are you mad that I didn't tell you?" she asked Nathan.

While he shook his head, he bit off a chunk of the bar. "I knew Dad wasn't my real dad. Lacey told me, remember?"

"I remember." Ivy's jaw was suddenly a little tight.

Theo waited for Nathan to ask more—such as why Theo hadn't seen him in all this time—but he continued to eat his breakfast as if this were an ordinary day.

"Are those bad men going to find us?" Nathan finally said.

Theo wished they'd stayed on the subject of fatherhood, but he hadn't expected Nathan just to forget the attack. "No. That's why we're in this house. If we have to stay here long, I'll have one of your uncles bring out some cereal for you."

"Thanks." He finished off the last bite of the granola bar and looked up at Theo. "Will you and my mom be together? You know, like some moms and dads?"

Theo was certain he had the same deer-in-the-headlights look as Ivy, but Ivy didn't seem to have trouble finding her voice. "No. But you will get to see Theo if that's what you want."

"Sure." Nathan stood and cleaned up after himself. "Can I go play a game on the computer now?"

Ivy nodded, and she seemed to release the breath she'd been holding when Nathan took off. However, he quickly stopped and whirled back around. "I think Aunt Jodi's a little sad. Because this was supposed to be the day she got married to Uncle Gabriel."

"I'll talk to her," Theo assured him. That was apparently all the answer he needed, because Nathan hurried to the bedroom.

Theo waited to see if Ivy would start to cry again, but she blew out another long breath and sat next to him. "I thought Nathan would take it harder than that."

Theo made a sound of agreement. And since she'd brought it up—and wasn't crying—he pushed the conversation a little. "When this is over, I want to see a whole lot more of Nathan. I want to get to know him."

She stared at him. "But what about your job? You're rarely around."

"True, but that could change. I've been a

joe for a long time, and the DEA would probably like to see me behind a desk for a while."

"You'd want to do that?" She made it sound as if he'd be jumping off a cliff.

Nothing so drastic, but it would be a total lifestyle change for him. One that Theo hadn't thought he'd ever want to make. Then again, he'd never thought he would have a son, either.

"I'm not walking away from Nathan," he warned her. "He'll get to know me as his father, the way he should have from the start."

He hadn't meant for that to sound so harsh, but it was hard to rein in the emotions when it came to the boy. Ivy held all the emotional cards here. She had the history and connection with their son. He was going to have to build it from the ground up.

"Gabriel, Jodi and Jameson will want to spend time with him, too," Theo went on. "After all, Nathan is their only nephew." And he waited for her to dismiss that or accept it.

One way or another, Ivy was going to have to accept it.

He didn't have to wait long. She gave another of those weary sighs. "I didn't plan to keep Nathan from my brothers or Jodi. Or from you. It all got mixed up into one giant mental mess. The murders. Our breakup. Jodi nearly dying. Gabriel and Jameson weren't in a good place mentally, and they had their hands full with the investigation. When I suspected I might be pregnant, I decided to leave." She paused. "They honestly didn't know about Nathan. I made sure they didn't know."

Because Gabriel and Jameson would have gone after her and tried to bring her home. He got that.

"And you didn't stay around, either," she reminded him.

No, he hadn't. "I had to get away, too." He'd had his own mental mess to deal with. "I kept thinking I should have been there to protect Jodi. I shouldn't have let that monster nearly knife her to death. That got mixed up with me being a suspect. Then my father's arrest."

Ivy stayed quiet a moment. "Do you think Travis is innocent?"

He couldn't give her a simple answer. Because there wasn't one. "I thought he was. Then Jodi and the rest of you started getting those threatening letters and emails. I'm a lawman, so I had to look at it from the angle that maybe the real killer was doing this so he could taunt you."

"Or it could be August trying to create doubt for his brother," she quickly pointed out.

Yes, that was more than possible. Still, he doubted his father would have gone along with a plan if it'd actually endangered either the Beckett children or Jodi and him. That meant there was still the possibility of a real killer out there or someone with a sick obsession about all of this.

Theo's phone buzzed, and he saw DEA agent Matt Krueger's name on the screen. He answered the call while he went to the window to have a look outside.

"Please tell me you found something about that militia raid I was asking about," Theo greeted.

Matt hesitated a moment. "Yes, that. I did go over everything, and I see what you mean about maybe the pieces not fitting. I'm thinking someone could have tipped off the militia about agents having infiltrated them."

That's what Theo had considered as well, but it still twisted at him to think that a fellow agent could have done that. "Is there any proof?"

"Maybe. I just went through the surveillance footage we have, and Wesley made a call about thirty minutes before the attack. Since he was using a prepaid cell, there's no way to trace it. Any idea who he called?"

"None." In fact, that was the point in the assignment, when he, Wesley and the agent who'd died—Ross Callahan—should have been keeping watch for an arms shipment that was about to come in.

"I think it's time for me to ask Wesley about this," Theo added. "I'll give him a call—"

"You haven't heard?" Matt interrupted.

"Heard what?" Theo asked.

"I just got the news a couple of minutes ago. Gabriel apparently took Wesley into custody. Don't know the details yet, but the sheriff found some kind of evidence to link Wesley to those dead gunmen."

Everything inside Theo went still. "What kind of evidence?"

"I'm not sure. Gabriel's holding that close to the vest. But Wesley claims that you set him up, that you're the one responsible for those gunmen who attacked last night."

Theo cursed. "And why the hell would I have done something like that?"

Matt hesitated again. "Wesley said you did it to get Ivy out of the way so you could get custody of your son."

Chapter Eight

Theo was still cursing under his breath after they got in the cruiser, and even though Ivy hadn't timed it, it'd been well over an hour since his intense phone conversation with Matt Krueger.

During that time, Wesley had accused Theo of attempted murder.

And that's why Theo had immediately started making plans to go to the sheriff's office in Blue River. He did that by arranging for Jameson to come out and stay with Nathan while the deputy, Cameron Doran, drove with Theo as backup into town. Theo and Cameron had been friends since childhood, and Theo trusted him. But Ivy made sure she was in on those plans, too, even though Theo had insisted it wasn't the right thing to do.

Heck, she wasn't sure it was the right thing,

either, but she did want to be there when Gabriel interrogated Wesley. And Lacey, as well. Gabriel had had to reschedule her interview so that her lawyer would be there with her.

"If Wesley's the one behind this," Theo said to her, "then you're not the target. That means there's no reason for you to be there."

Theo had already voiced several variations of that argument to get her to stay at the safe house, and it might be true. The investigation had certainly taken a strange turn, what with Wesley's accusations. Too bad that it might take them a long time to sort it out.

Time they didn't have.

Nathan was okay for now at the safe house with Jodi and Jameson, but Ivy hated the thought of him being shut away. Hated more that her little boy was in danger. Maybe they would get some answers, and soon, and put an end to that.

Theo continued to mumble profanity while he read a text. He did that while volleying glances all around them. So did Cameron while he drove them toward town. Thankfully, it was a rural road with no other traffic, so it should be easy to spot someone trying to follow them. Unfortunately, there were plenty of old ranch trails and even some thick woods between the safe house and Blue River. That's the reason Theo had wanted Cameron to make this drive with him.

"SAPD can't find a money trail for McKenzie and either of the dead gunmen," Theo relayed to her once he'd finished reading the text.

It was frustrating but something she'd expected. None of their known suspects would have left that kind of evidence behind.

"What about the phone call McKenzie made to Lacey?" she asked.

Theo shook his head. "SAPD can't even be sure McKenzie made that call. There were no prints on the phone. It'd been wiped clean."

Ivy huffed. "That means someone could have killed McKenzie and then used his phone to set up Lacey."

"Yep. And Lacey could have done it that way to throw suspicion off herself. That way, if her name did show up on any of McKenzie's other outgoing calls, then she could say she was being framed."

"And she might be," Ivy admitted. "If someone wants us dead, Lacey would be the perfect patsy since she has motive. Well, motive to go after Nathan and me, anyway. But the person behind this could plan to make it look as if the real target was caught in the middle." She paused. "Of course, we don't know who the 'real target' is."

Theo made a sound of agreement. "About how much money does Lacey think she lost out on with the inheritance?" he asked.

"Four million," she answered after a pause.

That got the reaction she expected. Shock. Yes, she'd married a rich, older man. Practically a cliché. But what was missing from that cliché was that Chad had loved her and had taken very good care of Nathan and her.

"Four million is a lot of motive for murder," Theo pointed out. "You said something about your late husband wanting Lacey to learn to be more responsible. I take it they clashed?"

"A lot. Lacey hated me right from the start and thought I was trying to replace her mother. She died of cancer when Lacey was just a little girl. I think she would have resented any woman her dad married, but it didn't help that she and I are so close in age. She probably would have called me a gold digger, but I had my own money."

Not as much as Chad, but it was close.

"Anyway, Chad divided his estate between Nathan and me," Ivy added. "He left Lacey only a small amount that'll remain in a trust until she's forty."

Theo shifted his position a little until their gazes connected. "Chad loved Nathan."

"He did, in his own way. More like an uncle's love than a father's." Chad had loved her, too, but Ivy figured she didn't need to spell that out. She especially didn't need to spell out that she'd never loved the man who had made her his wife.

"Good," he said under his breath just as his phone dinged again with another text message. The texts had been coming in at a steady rate since the earlier call from the DEA agent.

"Wesley brought my boss in on this," Theo read. "He's also demanding that Gabriel take me into custody."

She was betting her brother wasn't going to do that. Well, unless Wesley came up with some kind of evidence that would force Gabriel's hand.

Theo groaned softly. "I didn't do what Wesley said I did."

"I know," Ivy readily agreed. Theo turned toward her, fast, as if he hadn't expected her to dismiss the charges so easily. "You're not the sort to break the law," she added. "Well, not since you were sixteen."

The corner of his mouth lifted into a smile. One that lasted only a couple of seconds. But it was nice to see it even for that short time. It brought back memories of other smiles, of happier times.

That seemed a lifetime ago.

"My run-ins with the law were petty," he said. "And stupid."

"Yes. I remember the time you and your friends took my dad's tractor apart and re-assembled it in the hayloft. Must have taken you hours."

"All night," Theo admitted. "Your dad had warned me not to touch you when I took you out so I wanted to give him a little payback."

Well, it had certainly struck a nerve with her dad, that's for sure. But then her father had never liked Theo. Sherman had thought right from the start that Ivy could do a whole lot better than the likes of Theo Canton.

She hadn't.

In some ways, no man had ever lived up to him. And that wasn't an especially comforting thought. Things between Theo and her were tense. Maybe not as much as they had been just twenty-four hours earlier, but they were a long way from getting over their pasts.

Something they would have to do for Nathan's sake.

"Has anyone gotten in touch with your sister?" Cameron asked Ivy. "Because Lauren could be in danger, too."

Ivy nodded. "Jameson called her. She didn't answer her phone, but then she usually lets any calls from family go to voice mail."

She met Cameron's eyes in the rearview mirror and saw the flicker of emotion. It was gone in a flash and probably something he hadn't wanted her to see. But Ivy could guess what this was about. Cameron had once been in love with her kid sister, and the murders had torn them apart. Just as it'd done to Theo and her. Now, Lauren had built her life far away from Blue River. Far away from family and friends.

"Lauren is taking precautions in case this guy goes after her?" Theo pressed.

"She texted Jameson back and told him she'd be careful. She has a son now, so I'm sure she will do anything to protect him."

Theo glanced at Cameron, and even though neither man said anything, everyone knew that Lauren was still a raw nerve for Cameron. It probably hadn't helped that she'd gotten married and become a mom. A single mom, though, since her husband had died a little over a year ago. Or so Ivy had heard. Lauren hadn't exactly stayed in touch with her, either.

"So many lives got messed up that night the Becketts died," Cameron mumbled. "Lauren blamed me for a lot of that."

She had. And the blame was partially warranted. Cameron had been a rookie deputy at the time, along with being friends with Theo's family. Just a couple of hours before the murders, Cameron had run into Travis drunk outside the town's bar. He'd taken Travis's keys, but he hadn't arrested him for public intoxication. If Cameron had, then Travis would have been locked up, and he couldn't have committed two murders. She doubted Cameron would ever forgive himself for that.

And neither would Lauren.

"What the hell?" Cameron said, getting Ivy's attention. Theo, too.

She followed the deputy's gaze to the road ahead and spotted a blond-haired woman. Ivy didn't recognize her, but she was on the gravel shoulder, her hands in the air as if she were surrendering.

"You know her?" Theo immediately asked Cameron.

"No. She's not local. I have no idea why

she's in the road, but I don't think she's carrying a gun."

Ivy agreed, and since the woman was wearing a body-clinging cotton dress, it would have been hard for her to conceal a weapon. Not impossible, though, and that's probably why Theo motioned for Ivy to get down on the seat. She did, but not before trying to get a better glimpse of whatever the heck was going on.

"You see anyone else?" Theo again, and the question was directed at Cameron.

"No," the deputy repeated, and he slowed the cruiser to a crawl. "Keep the windows up," he instructed—probably because they were bullet-resistant. "She doesn't have on any shoes, and her feet are bleeding. It's possible she got stranded by the river or something."

It was the possibility of that "or something" that troubled Ivy, and when Cameron brought the cruiser to a stop, Ivy could see the woman. She still had her hands in the air. And looked dazed. Her hair was a tangled mess, and while Ivy didn't have a view of her feet, there was also blood and what appeared to be a bruise on the right side of her face. What she didn't do was rush forward.

Strange.

After all, they were in a Blue River Sheriff's Department cruiser that was clearly marked, and both Cameron and Theo were wearing their badges.

Cameron called for an ambulance for backup. He did that because he probably wanted a cop to go with her to the hospital. Then he lowered his window just a fraction.

"Are you all right?" he asked her, sounding very much like the lawman that he was.

She shook her head. "I think I was kidnapped."

Yes, definitely strange. A person should know for certain if they were kidnapped or not, but maybe someone had drugged her. Whoever had done that perhaps caused that injury to her face.

"What's your name?" Cameron pressed. "And who kidnapped you?"

Another shake of her head, and a hoarse sob tore from her mouth. "I'm not supposed to be here."

Cameron huffed. "Then where are you supposed to be, and who brought you here?"

Several moments crawled by, and while Theo was watching her, he continued to glance around. Ivy wanted to help him do that, but she knew it would only make him more on edge if she did.

"I'm sorry," the woman said.

"For what?" Cameron snapped.

But she didn't get a chance to answer. That's because a shot cracked through the air and the bullet slammed right into the woman's chest.

THEO DIDN'T SEE the shooter, but he certainly heard the bullet. And hc had no trouble seeing the damage it did.

The blonde made a sharp sound of pain, clutched her chest and dropped to the ground. Theo didn't think she was dead, but she soon would be. The blood was already spreading across the front of her dress.

"We have gunfire," Cameron said to whoever he had called. Probably Gabriel, who would in turn have to hold off on sending in an ambulance.

"Can you pull her into the cruiser?" Ivy asked, as she sat up to get a better look at their surroundings.

Theo was already debating doing just that. It would be a risk, but at this point anything they did would be. The woman had clearly been drugged and was probably part of a trap to get them to stop. It'd worked, but if she was truly innocent in all of this, she could die.

He didn't have long to dwell on his decision, though, because there was another sound. A second shot, and this one didn't go into the woman.

It blasted into the window just above Ivy's head. The glass held though it did crack, but it wouldn't hold for long if the shooter kept firing into it.

And that's exactly what he did.

"You see the gunman?" Cameron asked.

"No. But he must be in those trees across the road." The woods were thick there, and even though the morning sun was bright, the light wasn't making it through the dense branches and underbrush.

Who the hell was doing this?

Theo didn't know, but at the moment their best bet for telling them that was lying on the ground, bleeding out.

"Can you open the window on the front passenger's side just enough to return fire?" Theo said to Cameron.

Cameron glanced back at him, and he didn't look any more certain of this than Theo felt. "You're going to get the woman in the cruiser?"

Theo hoped he didn't regret this, but he nodded. "Get down on the floor," he instructed Ivy. That would not only get her a few inches farther from the window, it would free up the seat so he could drag the woman inside.

"Please be careful," Ivy said, the fear and emotion thick in her voice. It was in her expression, too, and Theo would have liked the time to assure her this was the right thing to do, but there was nothing he could say that would take the worry off her face.

Hell, he was worried, too.

Not for himself and Cameron. But for Ivy. If she was indeed the target, then all of this could be designed to get to her.

Several more shots came at them, each tearing through the window next to Ivy. Obviously, the gunmen were focusing on her. Or else the thug wanted them to think she was the focus. Theo wasn't going to take any of this at face value.

Cameron kept the engine running, but he moved to the passenger's window, lowered it just enough to stick out the barrel of his gun and looked at Theo to give him the go-ahead.

Theo nodded.

And Cameron fired.

The moment the deputy did that, Theo

threw open his door, and he glanced over his shoulder to make sure Ivy was still down. She was. But she was watching him and mumbling something. A prayer, from the sound of it.

Theo moved as fast as he could and hoped he didn't do any more damage to the injured woman when he latched onto her arm and started dragging her to the cruiser. The shots didn't stop. In fact, the gunman picked up the pace, and this time he fired at Theo. The bullets slammed into the ground, kicking up the gravel that was on the shoulder.

The woman cried out in pain, and that's when Theo realized she'd been hit again. This time in the shoulder. Theo hadn't needed any more incentive to move as fast as he could, but that did it.

And he got some help.

Unwanted help.

Ivy scrambled over the floor of the cruiser, and the moment Theo was back at the door, she reached out and helped him drag the woman inside. By doing that, she put herself in even greater danger. Later, Theo would tell her what a stupid thing that was to do, but then he saw the bullets slam into the ground where he'd just been. If Ivy hadn't helped, he could be dead.

"Get us out of here," Theo said to Cameron as soon as he had the woman on the seat.

Cameron was already moving to do that, and as soon as he was back behind the wheel, he hit the accelerator.

The cruiser sped away as the bullets continued to rip through the window.

Chapter Nine

Ivy tried to force herself to focus. There was a lot going on at the Blue River sheriff's office, but she couldn't grasp it all. That probably had to do with the spent adrenaline that had left her exhausted.

Too bad the exhaustion hadn't stopped the sound of the gunshots from echoing in her head. Or stopped the fear that was still racing through her. Mercy, she wanted that gone most of all, because at the moment most of those fears were for her son.

The gunman who'd fired those shots had gotten away. And it wasn't as if no one had looked for him. Gabriel had sent out two deputies almost immediately, but by the time they'd arrived, there'd been no sign of him. That meant the man was out there, probably waiting to attack. Or worse, waiting to follow them to the safe house where Nathan was with Jameson and Jodi.

"How did the gunman even know we'd be on that stretch of the road?" she asked. It wasn't the first time she'd wanted to know that, and Ivy didn't direct the question at anyone in particular.

Theo, however, put away his phone after making his latest call and went to her. He skimmed his hand down her arm, probably a gesture to try to comfort her, but Ivy figured nothing much was going to soothe her right now.

"There are only two roads leading into Blue River," Theo reminded her. "There could have been a gunman on both."

Yes. And that meant there could have been another woman or hostage to force them into stopping. Or coerced. If so, Ivy hoped they found the person, and the thugs hadn't done to him or her what they'd done to the woman they'd encountered. She couldn't imagine that someone had volunteered to be shot as part of the plan to lure her out into the open.

"Jameson is on full alert," Theo went on. "If anyone tries to get near the safe house, he'll let us know."

She didn't doubt that. Didn't doubt that her

brother and Jodi would be vigilant. But this monster could still get to them.

"I just want to rush back to Nathan," she said. Ivy cursed the tears that she was having to blink back. Tears weren't going to help this, and they only put more stress on Theo because it was obvious he was concerned about her. Ivy quickly waved that off. "But I don't want to lead the guy straight to Nathan, either."

Theo nodded to let her know they were on the same page about that. Actually, they were on the same page about several things, and it wasn't all related to the investigation. The attraction that kept rearing its head and the fact that they would do anything to protect their son.

"Any updates on the woman who was shot?" Ivy asked. Maybe if she talked about the investigation, she could get her mind off Nathan. "Or Wesley?"

Even though the agent was still in the building, he was in an interview room with Gabriel and Theo's boss. Gabriel hadn't wanted Theo to be part of that, maybe because he now had Theo on his suspect list. Even if he hadn't been a suspect, though, it could still compromise things since Wesley and he were fellow agents.

"There's nothing on Wesley," Theo answered, "but whatever he's telling Gabriel is a lie. I didn't have anything to do with this."

"I know," she assured him, and it wasn't lip service. Theo wouldn't do anything to harm Nathan and her. And no, that wasn't the attraction talking. Now, though, she might have to convince Gabriel of Theo's innocence—something she hadn't tried to do ten years ago. That was a mistake she didn't intend to make again.

"As for the woman, I just talked to a doctor at the hospital, and she's still alive," Theo went on. "That's the good news. But she'd been heavily drugged, and one of the gunshot wounds is serious. She's in surgery."

Ivy already knew the woman hadn't said anything in the cruiser on the drive to the hospital because she was unconscious through the entire trip. She also hadn't moved at all when the medics had taken her away on a gurney. Of course, Theo, Cameron and Ivy hadn't waited around to talk to the doctor. It was too dangerous. Instead, Theo had rushed them to the sheriff's office, where they'd been for the past hour.

"The woman didn't have an ID on her," Theo went on, "so we're not positive who she is. But she matches the description of a woman, Belinda Travers, who went missing the night before. From McKenzie's club."

That got Ivy's attention. "She knew McKenzie?"

He lifted his shoulder. "It's possible she just went into the bar, one of the hired guns saw her and decided to use her as bait."

So she could be innocent in all of this. It sickened Ivy to think of how many people had been hurt—or could be hurt—and they didn't know why or by who.

"They did a bug sweep of the sheriff's office and the rest of the building while we were at the safe house," Theo said a moment later. "And they found one."

She could have sworn her heart skipped a couple of beats, and the panic came. It was so strong that she nearly bolted for the door so she could go after Nathan. Theo took hold of her arm and anchored her in place.

"It was by the dispatch desk," he explained, "and it's been removed."

The dispatch desk was also Reception. That meant anyone who'd come into the building could have put it there. Heck, it could have been there for weeks or longer.

"Remember, we whispered whenever we talked about the safe house," Theo reminded her.

Yes, they had. Maybe that had been enough to keep those thugs away from her son.

"Come on." Theo still had hold of her, and he got her moving toward the hall. "We can go to the break room and maybe you can get some rest."

Rest was out, but her legs suddenly felt too wobbly to stand. Maybe she could at least sit down and wait for news about when they could return to the safe house. However, they only made it a few steps down the hall when the interview room door opened, and Gabriel stepped out. Judging from her brother's expression, things hadn't gone well. She got further confirmation of that when Wesley and the other man came out.

Dwight Emory.

Even though Ivy hadn't met the man, she knew this was Theo and Wesley's boss. He didn't look especially pleased, either, but then, one of his agents—Wesley—was accusing a fellow agent—Theo—of a crime.

"Well?" Theo prompted when no one said anything.

"We're sorting it out," Emory answered.

"We're not close to sorting it out," Wesley snarled. He nailed a glare to Theo. "How could you do this to me? We've been partners for years. Friends," he amended. "At least I thought we were, and then you start asking questions. You're treating me like a criminal."

Theo huffed, and his hands went on his hips. "Seems to me you're the one who said I wanted Ivy out of the way so I could get Nathan."

"Don't you?" Wesley challenged.

"No." And Theo moved closer to her, sliding his arm around her waist. He probably did that because she wasn't looking so steady, but it was also a signal to Wesley and Emory that the old baggage between them wasn't as toxic as it had once been.

Ivy wasn't sure when that'd happened exactly. Maybe around the time Theo had been trying to save her life.

Theo volleyed glances between Emory and Gabriel. "What kind of proof did Wesley produce to make an accusation like that against me?"

"A CI told me," Wesley volunteered.

Ivy wasn't sure who gave Wesley the flattest look, but Gabriel, Theo and even Emory weren't jumping to embrace the so-called evidence.

"We're trying to find the CI now," Emory finally said. "If he confirms Wesley's claim, then we'll still have to consider the source." Emory looked at her then. "As you can imagine, CIs aren't always truthful, and this could be a situation of someone wanting to get back at Theo."

"Yeah, Wesley could be doing that," Theo insisted. "Because he might want to get suspicion off himself."

Wesley howled out a protest, but Gabriel made a sound of agreement. "I got the security footage of McKenzie's bar. It's grainy and there are only a few good camera angles—"

"I didn't go there to pay off anybody," Wesley interrupted.

Ivy glanced at Theo to see if he knew what any of this was about, but he only shook his head. "What happened on that footage?" Theo asked Gabriel.

Her brother took a deep breath first. "When Wesley entered the bar, he took out an envelope from his jacket pocket. And, yeah, he was wearing a jacket despite the fact that it was ninety degrees outside. It gets grainy when

Wesley goes to a booth in the corner, but it appears he gives the envelope to a known thug by the name of Nixon Vaughn."

Oh, mercy. That wasn't good, and Ivy immediately wondered if this Vaughn was a hired gun. Maybe the very one who'd attacked them today and shot that woman.

"He's not on payroll for the DEA or any other agency," Emory added.

Theo's jaw was very tight when he turned to Wesley. "Did you pay off Vaughn?"

Wesley's jaw wasn't exactly relaxed, either. "Yes. Because you told me to."

A burst of air left Theo's mouth. "No, I didn't. And what makes you think I did?"

"I got a text from you." Wesley muttered some profanity under his breath. "You said to give Vaughn five hundred bucks, and that you'd pay me back. You said Vaughn had info about the threatening letters the Becketts had been getting. So I gave Vaughn the money, but he said he didn't know anything about the Becketts."

"The text came from a burner cell," Emory provided.

"Theo uses burners all the time," Wesley snapped.

As the daughter and sister of cops, Ivy

knew what a burner was. It was a prepaid phone that couldn't be traced. Theo probably did use them for his job, but in this case some-one had used it to set him up.

To maybe set up Wesley, too.

But why would someone have done that?

Maybe the person hoped to get both Theo and Wesley thrown off the case. If so, it wasn't working. Theo wasn't going to let this go whether he was officially on the investiga-tion or not, and she doubted Wesley would just walk away, either.

"Obviously, I need to look into this fur-ther," Emory said. "But at this point, Wesley is going back to his office, and, Theo, the sheriff and I decided you should continue with pro-tective custody for Ivy and her son."

Emory hesitated before "her son," as if he weren't sure whether to include Theo in that parent label or not.

Theo thanked his boss, though it wasn't a very enthusiastic one, and he shot Wesley a glare before he started with her toward the break room. Both Emory and Wesley walked away, but Gabriel stayed put.

"Your dad's lawyer called first thing this morning," Gabriel said, stopping Theo in his tracks. "August visited Travis and told him about Nathan. Travis asked if he could see him."

"No," Theo answered without giving even a moment's thought. Then he shook his head, cursed. "Even if it were safe to take Nathan out, I don't want him visiting a prison."

Both Gabriel and Ivy added a sound of agreement, though they were in tricky territory here. Nathan was Travis's only grandchild, but since Travis was also a convicted killer of her own parents, then Ivy didn't want to give Travis the chance to say anything to the boy that could possibly upset him. Nathan had already been through enough, and she had told him only a few sketchy details about her folks' deaths. She certainly hadn't told him that his grandfather was a convicted murderer.

"The lawyer said he could set up a Skype call with all of you and Travis," Gabriel added. "I told him if you were interested in that, you'd let him know. I didn't tell him that hell might freeze over before that happened."

Theo smiled, muttered a thanks. He turned to get her moving but then stopped again. "What about Jodi's and your wedding? You were supposed to be getting married today."

"Yeah." Gabriel sounded and looked disappointed. "It's still on hold. Jodi and I are okay with that."

They no doubt were okay, but Ivy hated that their plans had been derailed because of some sick monster who wanted at least some of them dead. Of course, all the danger seemed to point to Theo, Nathan and her. At least Jodi didn't seem to be in the path of a killer. After she had already survived not one but two attacks, Ivy didn't want her soon-to-be sister-in-law to go through anything else like that.

Theo led her to the break room, such that it was. It had a microwave, small fridge and a beat-up leather sofa. Theo had her sit, got her a bottle of water from the fridge and then took out his phone. At first she thought he was going to make another of those calls to get updates on the investigation, but when he put it on speaker, she heard Jameson's voice.

"How's Nathan?" Theo immediately asked.

"Fine. Jodi and he are watching a movie. Are Ivy and you okay?"

Since Jameson knew about the attack, he was aware that they hadn't been injured. Not physically, anyway. "I think Ivy will be a lot better if she can talk to Nathan." And Theo handed her the phone.

Other than the initial call to the safe house

after they'd arrived at the sheriff's office, Ivy hadn't considered talking to Nathan. She hadn't wanted him to hear the fear in her voice, but the moment her son came onto the line, that fear vanished.

"Uncle Jameson taught me to play poker," Nathan proudly announced.

"Kiddie poker," Jameson corrected.

Ivy figured it was the real deal since her brother favored that particular game, and she honestly didn't mind. Nathan sounded excited as if this were some kind a treat, and that was better than the alternative. Plus, he was getting to spend time with his uncle, something that Nathan hadn't ever had a chance to do.

"Aunt Jodi can't cook at all," Nathan went on. "She burned the toast and cut her finger when she was trying to make a sandwich. But Uncle Jameson can make grilled cheese and popcorn."

"Hey, I'm giving him some fruit, too," Jameson called out.

"Yeah, fruit and chocolate milk," Nathan concurred.

Again, her son sounded happy. "I miss you," Ivy told him. "But maybe it won't be long before Theo...your dad and I can come back."

"Okay. Can you bring some pizza?"

Ivy had to smile. "I'll try." Even after all the food that was just mentioned, she wasn't surprised that Nathan had pizza on the mind. It was his favorite. "See you soon, sweetheart."

Even though she was so glad she'd been able to speak to Nathan, the moment she ended the call, Ivy felt the loss. She had spent so little time away from him that even this short while felt like an eternity.

"I've missed so much," Theo said.

She looked at him, saw the loss on his face, too, but it was far worse than hers. After all, she'd had Nathan all these years that he hadn't. It hadn't been a decision to keep Nathan from Theo. At first, it'd been because of the rift between them and then because she couldn't find him. But after seeing Theo's raw expression, Ivy wished she'd done more.

Theo had indeed missed a lot.

She stood and went to him, and though it wasn't a smart thing to do, she pulled him into her arms. At least that's what she started to do, but Theo did some pulling of his own. Maybe it was the emotion of the moment or the fact that they'd just escaped death. Either way, it was as if he snapped. He dragged her to him.

And he kissed her.

It had been ten years since Theo's mouth

had been on hers, but the memories—and the feelings—came flooding back. Ivy hadn't especially needed a kiss to remind her why Theo and she had been together in the first place, but the heat was just as hot as it had been back when they were teenagers.

He'd been the first boy to kiss her, and she had lost her virginity to him. And yes, there was still enough attraction there that she remembered exactly why that had happened. Theo had had her hormonal number then, and he still had it now.

She heard herself make a sound of pleasure, something she often did whenever she was around Theo, and the sound only increased when he deepened the kiss. He added some nice body pressure, too, with his chest moving right against her breasts. It didn't take long for her body to recall just how good the pleasure could be. It also didn't take long for Ivy to find herself wanting more.

Theo was obviously on that "more" page as well because he turned her, moving her so that her back was against the wall. He made the adjustment with her, still touching her with his body. Especially one part of him. In the maneuvering, his thigh ended up between her legs, and the pressure started to build there.

She broke the kiss so she could breathe, and when she pulled back a few inches, Ivy was staring right into his eyes. Those eyes had always had her number, too, and it didn't seem to matter that ten years had passed, because her body was on fire. Still, she forced herself to remember they were in the break room where anyone could come walking in at any second. No way would Gabriel approve of such a thing, and she shouldn't approve of it, either, since they had so many more important things they should be doing.

She repeated that last part to herself. It didn't help. Every inch of her was still zinging from the kiss.

"I should say I'm sorry for that." Theo's voice was husky and deep, and it did nothing to cool her off. It also did nothing to make her want an apology from him or even regret that it'd happened.

But she should regret it.

There were still a lot of unsettled things between Theo and her. Added to that, someone was trying to kill them. The last thing she should have been doing was kissing him. Or wanting to kiss him again.

Which she did.

Ivy might have done just that, too, but the

break room door opened, and Gabriel came in. Theo and she immediately stepped apart. She was certain they looked guilty, and equally certain that her brother was aware of what'd happened between them. And yes, Gabriel scowled in a way that only a big brother could manage when he believed his kid sister was making a mistake.

The same mistake she'd made a decade ago.

"I would offer to give you a moment," Gabriel grumbled, sarcasm in his voice, "but this is important."

That got her heart pumping. "Is Nathan okay?"

"This isn't about Nathan. A courier just arrived with some very interesting things that you should take a look at." He turned, headed back toward his office and said the rest from over his shoulder. "Cameron is calling Lacey now to get her in here. She's in town, staying at the inn, so it shouldn't take her long to get here. Once you see this, you'll know why I might have to arrest her."

Chapter Ten

Theo forced his attention on Gabriel and what he'd just told them. It should have been an easy thing to do, what with the investigation and the danger, but he first had to shake off the effects of that kiss.

What the hell had he been thinking?

He had no idea, but Theo knew for a fact which of his body parts had encouraged him to do that, and it was the very part of him that could make stupid choices just like that one. Later, he would owe Ivy that apology he'd skirted around, but it would have to wait for now. Clearly, Gabriel had something important to show them.

"The courier is still here," Gabriel said to them as they walked into his office. "I've put him in an interview room so I can find out more about who had him deliver this. The envelope just has the name John Smith, no address, and the courier only had a vague description of the guy."

It was probably vague because the person hadn't wanted to draw attention to himself. Or could have even been wearing a disguise. If the person who'd attacked them was behind this, he or she probably wouldn't have done something so stupid as approaching the courier themselves. They would have hired someone to do that. Someone who couldn't be traced back to them.

Theo figured Gabriel was going to clarify all of this very soon, but for now he had one big question. "What does Lacey have to do with this?"

"Maybe everything." Gabriel tipped his head to his desk where Theo saw not only a manila envelope, but the item that was lying next to it. It was in a clear plastic evidence bag.

A silver watch.

Hell. What was going on here? The watch face was ordinary, but the band had small copper insets. Theo had only seen one other watch like that.

It had belonged to Ivy and Gabriel's father. Ivy gasped, pressed her fingers against her mouth and took a step back. She shook her head. "Is that… Dad's?"

"According to this, it is," Gabriel said. He seemed to be struggling with seeing the watch, too. Of course, it didn't help that Sherman had been wearing it at the time of his murder.

And that the killer had taken the watch—probably as some kind of sick trophy.

The watch hadn't been found on Theo's father, though. For that matter, neither had the knife that'd murdered Sherman and his wife.

"It's a lab report," Gabriel said. He didn't touch the paper next to the envelope, but he pointed to it. "Someone claims to have had prints and trace run on the watch." He paused, his forehead bunching up. "There's a small amount of blood. A DNA match to Dad."

Ivy didn't gasp again, but she made a soft, strangling sound, groped around for the chair that was behind her and sank down onto it. "Where's it been this whole time?"

Gabriel shook his head. "The lab report doesn't mention that. Of course, my theory was that Travis had hidden it somewhere. Or ditched it like he did the knife. And maybe he did."

Someone had found the knife, though, hidden it away and then tried to use it to kill Jodi. That'd happened only a month earlier. But the person who'd done that was dead and couldn't have been the one to send the watch.

"I'll have it tested, of course," Gabriel continued a moment later. "Not just for blood but also to verify the partial prints that this report says were on the watch band."

"Prints?" Ivy repeated. "Whose?"

Theo figured it was Travis's prints. Since Sherman's blood had been found on Travis's shirt, it wouldn't be much of a stretch for the prints to belong to his father, as well.

Apparently they didn't, though.

"They're Lacey's," Gabriel said.

Oh, man. That explained why Gabriel had wanted Ivy's stepdaughter brought in, but that was about all it explained.

"Lacey was twenty when our parents were killed," Ivy pointed out. "And she didn't know them. She didn't even live close to Blue River when the murders happened."

"That's exactly why I want to talk to her," Gabriel continued. "If those are really her prints, then she must have touched the watch at some point—either at the time of the murder or afterward."

"*Afterward* could mean someone is setting

her up," Theo pointed out. But then there was a problem with that. "Who had the watch to be able to do something like that, and why set up Lacey this way? If someone wanted to tie her to the attacks, there would have been an easier way to do that by just creating a fake money trail."

Obviously, neither Gabriel nor Ivy had answers for that, and if it was a setup, Lacey might not know it, either. But it could mean she'd come in contact with someone who'd been present at the murders. *Could.*

Theo hoped Ivy didn't take this the wrong way, but he had to ask. "Is it possible that your late husband knew your parents?"

She shook her head. But then she paused. "I honestly never asked him. All of that was still so raw and painful when I met Chad, and he seemed to sense that I didn't want to talk about it."

Theo looked at Gabriel, who was already taking out his phone. "I'll see if Chad's name came up at any point during the investigation or the check of the old police records."

That brought Ivy to her feet. "You can't think Chad killed them." She didn't seem to have any doubts about that. "Because he was a gentle man. He definitely wasn't a killer."

Theo took her hand and had her sit again. "I believe you, but it's possible he had some connection to my father. He might have known him, might have sympathized with the feud that was going on between the Becketts and the Cantons. Yeah, it's a long shot," he quickly added, "but we're working with nothing but long shots here."

And that meant Theo might have to talk to Travis after all. Not to have him meet Nathan. Not a chance. But rather to start ruling out any association he could have possibly had with Chad.

"How'd you meet Chad?" Gabriel asked the moment he ended his call.

She narrowed her eyes a little at her brother. Obviously, she wasn't pleased that her late husband was coming into question. Probably because it was too hard to wrap her mind around the fact that she might have been living with the man who'd had some part in her parents' death. And maybe he didn't. Again, this was a long shot.

"I met him at a livestock auction near Houston," Ivy finally answered. "I'd just bought a small place and wanted to buy a horse. Chad sat next to me, and when Nathan started fuss-ing, he started making funny faces at him and got him to stop."

For reasons Theo didn't want to explore, hearing that caused him to scowl. He figured what he was feeling was some old-fashioned jealousy, but hell, it was hard to hear of any man having that kind of interaction with his son when he hadn't had the chance to even see the baby.

Hard to hear about Ivy being with another man, too.

That kiss was responsible for him feeling that. And in this case, the jealousy didn't make a lick of sense. He'd been with other women since Ivy, but then, he hadn't married any of them. In fact, he hadn't even gotten past the casual sex stage. Theo had always blamed that on his job, but after that kiss with Ivy, he knew that his feelings for her were still there, and they had probably been playing into it even after all these years.

Ivy pushed her hair from her face, looked away. "After we met at the auction, Chad asked me out for coffee, and eventually I went…four months later."

So Ivy hadn't exactly jumped at the chance to be with another man. Not that Theo believed she had. Nathan had been nearly a year old when she'd married Chad, and that meant by then Theo had been out of her life for almost two years. She'd moved on. But she'd moved on with a man who could have some connection to the Beckett murders.

"If Chad had known my parents or had anything to do with that watch, why would he have asked me out?" Ivy questioned. "Why would he have married me? Because I can promise you that he never asked a question about my parents, and he certainly never tried to hurt me. So you're wasting your time trying to link Chad to Lacey's prints on that watch."

"You're wasting your time to link me to it, too," Lacey said.

The woman came into the doorway. Cameron was right behind her, and judging from the deputy's frustrated expression, he'd been trying to hold her back.

Lacey aimed glares at all of them, including Cameron, and her glare was still in place when her attention landed on the watch. "That's why you brought me in here?" she asked Gabriel.

Gabriel gave her a glare of his own. "Your prints are on it. Why?"

Theo carefully watched her expression, and if she was the least bit concerned about the accusations against her, she didn't show it.

Instead, she shrugged. "About a week or so ago, I was at the mall, and when I came out, that watch was lying on the hood of my car. I picked it up. I figured someone walking by had found it, thought it was mine and left it for me."

Theo didn't glare, but he was certain he looked skeptical. Because he was. "How'd the watch get from you to here?" he demanded.

"How should I know? I tossed it on the ground, got in my car and left. I didn't want to leave it on the hood because I thought it might hit my windshield and chip the glass."

"And you didn't think it was suspicious that someone would put a watch on your car?" Ivy asked. There was skepticism in her voice, too.

Lacey hadn't seemed to object too much to Theo's question, but she clearly didn't like Ivy's. "No, because like I said, I thought someone believed it was mine. Obviously, it's not my style, and it belongs to a man. I don't even have a current boyfriend."

If Lacey was telling the truth, then someone indeed had set her up. But Theo wasn't convinced that it'd been the truth that had come out of Lacey's mouth.

"Did you see anyone near your vehicle before you spotted the watch?" Gabriel pressed.

"No. Now, what's this about? Why is that watch so blasted important?"

"It belonged to my father," Ivy answered after everyone paused. "It went missing the night of his murder."

Now Lacey had a reaction. Her eyes widened, and she shook her head. "Oh, no. You're not going to try to pin that on me. It's bad enough that I'm stuck in this cowpoke town because the sheriff here thinks I might be behind the attacks to kill the likes of you. I won't have you accusing me of your parents' murders."

"How about your father?" Theo asked, ignoring the insults Lacey had peppered into her comments. "Could Chad have killed them?" He knew that wasn't going to earn him a kind look from Ivy. It didn't.

Lacey howled out a protest, but she didn't limit it to just Theo. She snapped toward Ivy, too. "You're behind this, aren't you? You think if you can get me out of the way, then I can't get what's rightfully mine."

Ivy blew out a long breath and stood, facing Lacey head-on. "I'm not behind this. If I'd found my father's watch, I would have given it to the cops because it might have some kind of evidence on it. I darn sure wouldn't have put it on your car, knowing that you could toss it."

That didn't seem to soothe Lacey any. The veins in her neck were practically bulging, and her nostrils were flared. "Please. You'd do anything to stop me from getting my father's money."

"Not anything," Ivy argued. "But there is something I can do to make sure my son is safe, and I did it. I had a lawyer redo my will. Since I'm trustee of Nathan's inheritance, I can make decisions about that, too. So if anything happens to Nathan and me, all of your father's money will go to charity."

The color drained from Lacey's face, and she looked at Theo for confirmation of that. He had no idea if it was true or not, but he nodded. "This way, you have no motive to come after our son."

"I never tried to kill him!" she shouted. Then she snapped back to Ivy. "You have no right to a single penny of my dad's money."

"Neither do you." Ivy huffed again, and Theo could see she was having to wrestle with her own temper. "Look, I would give you the money but your father asked me not to do that. It was his dying wish, something he told me many times over, and I'm going to do what he wanted."

Good call, because at this point just giving Lacey the money might not put an end to the danger. It seemed to Theo that Lacey wanted Ivy and Nathan completely out of the picture.

"My father loved me," the woman stated through clenched teeth.

"And he knew you," Ivy agreed. "He didn't think you were responsible enough to handle another large sum of money. Plus, he knew you wouldn't share it with me."

"Because it wasn't your money to have! You brainwashed my father. You got him to fall for you because he'd always wanted a son. Well, your brat kid isn't his son and never will be."

"No, because he's my son." Theo probably shouldn't have blurted that out, but Ivy wasn't the only one having to put a choke hold on her temper. He started to address the brat comment but decided against it. He'd already said too much.

"Like I care whose kid he is," Lacey grumbled. "This isn't over," she added to Ivy, and she turned as if to leave.

"No, it's not," Gabriel agreed. "And you're not going anywhere just yet." He ignored her protest and went into the hall, motioning for

Cameron to join them. "I need you to continue this interview with Miss Vogel, and if she refuses, lock her up. Based on what I have here, we won't have any trouble getting a court order."

Lacey fired glances at all of them. "You'll be sorry for this," she spat out, and she slung off Cameron's grip when he took hold of her arm.

However, Lacey didn't head out the front door, something Theo had thought she might try to do. She followed Cameron to his desk.

Gabriel stepped back in his office and shut the door. "You think she's lying?" he asked Theo and Ivy.

"I don't know," Theo admitted when Ivy shook her head. "But I don't trust her."

Both Gabriel and Ivy made sounds of agreement to that.

"Who could have left that watch for her?" Ivy asked, but she didn't wait for them to answer. "August, maybe? I know he wasn't at our old house the night of the murders, but maybe Travis gave it to him?"

No, August hadn't been at either the Beckett or the Canton house. Instead, he'd been with a woman one town over, and she'd provided him with an alibi for the time of the murders. That didn't mean, though, that August hadn't run into Travis later, since Theo's father hadn't been found until the following morning. Those were a lot of hours when a transfer like that could have taken place, and there was no way August would have volunteered that Travis had had the watch because it would have added another nail to his conviction for the murders.

"If Travis gave him the watch, August wouldn't have turned it over to Gabriel," Theo pointed out. But Theo had some trouble finishing that theory. "Why wouldn't August have planted the watch on someone who's a more plausible suspect, someone we would actually believe could have killed your parents if my father hadn't done it? Or he could have just tossed it in the river, where it probably would have never been found."

Obviously, Theo wasn't the only one having trouble coming up with a reason for August to do this.

"Now, Wesley—yes," Theo went on. "I can see an angle for him on this. If he'd somehow managed to get the watch, then he could have used it to frame Lacey so it would take suspicion off him."

"How would Wesley have gotten the watch, though?" Ivy asked.

Theo had the answer for this one. "Wesley was around during the murder investigation. In fact, he was a San Antonio cop then, and a group of them came out to help comb the area when everyone was looking for Travis. He could have found the watch then."

That didn't explain, though, why a cop would have kept something like that, but maybe Wesley had been dirty even back then. If so, he'd certainly kept his dirty deeds hidden away.

"There's a third theory, though," Theo continued a moment later. One that he hated to even consider. "Someone could be playing a cat-and-mouse game with us. Maybe a person my father has somehow managed to hire." He paused, not really wanting to consider this one as well, but they needed to look at all of the possibilities. However, it was Gabriel who finished that train of thought for him.

"Or your father could be innocent, and the real killer is out there," Gabriel said.

None of them believed that. Or at least they didn't want to believe it. Because if it was true, it would turn this investigation—and their lives—upside down. Again. It also meant

Theo had no way of protecting Ivy from a nameless, faceless monster who could have already butchered at least two people and had plenty of others in his or her sight.

Maybe even their son.

If this was truly someone wanting to spill Beckett blood, then Nathan could be a target. Of course, a killer could also use the boy to draw out Ivy and Theo. And it could work, since both of them would lay down their lives for the boy.

Theo hadn't intended to do it, but he slid his hand over Ivy's shoulder. Gabriel noticed, too. But then he was also the one who'd walked in on Ivy and him shortly after that kiss. Judging from Gabriel's expression, he was about to dole out some big brother advice. Maybe even a big brother warning. However, his phone rang before he could do that.

Theo kept his hand in place, and Ivy looked up at him. Their gazes connected for just a second before Gabriel interrupted them.

"It's the doctor who performed surgery on the injured woman." Gabriel put the call on speaker.

Theo braced himself for the doc to say the woman was dead. That would be tragic not only because she might be truly innocent in all of this, but also because they would lose their chance to question her.

"She's awake," the doctor announced. "And she says her name is Belinda Travers."

So she was the woman who'd gone missing from McKenzie's place. "Did she say anything else?" Theo asked at the same moment Gabriel said, "How soon can I talk to her?"

"Give it another hour," the doctor answered. "By then, she should be a little more alert. And as for the other question—yes, she told me something else. She said someone kidnapped her from a bar. She doesn't know the person who did that, but the reason she was there was to meet August Canton."

Chapter Eleven

Ivy wanted nothing more than to go back to the safe house so she could see Nathan. But there was no way her brother could spare the manpower right now. No way that Theo would let Ivy and him drive back there alone, either. Not after the other attack on the road and with the possibility of hired thugs still being in the area.

So she paced the hall in front of Gabriel's office. Waited.

And worried.

Gabriel had already questioned the courier and hadn't uncovered anything new, but her brother was definitely hoping to learn something from the watch, which he'd already sent for processing. Also to learn something from August. Once the man came in, that is. August had some answering to do over Belinda's accusations that she'd been at McKenzie's bar to meet him.

At least Lacey and Wesley wouldn't be around. Or rather they shouldn't be. It was unnerving enough having August return, and Ivy didn't especially want to be under the same roof with all three of their suspects.

The worries kept coming, too. Because the greatest danger might not be with August, Lacey or Wesley. Gabriel had mentioned the possibility of Travis being innocent, and if by some serious long shot he actually was, then God knew who'd killed her parents. But whoever it was could want her and the rest of her family dead.

Not exactly a reassuring thought.

That could explain why she and other members of her family had been getting those threatening letters over the years. There'd been details in some of those letters—such as her mother's necklace being taken—and the police had purposely kept those out of the reports. It'd been a way of putting a lid on false confessions. So the person who'd written those threats had either managed to hack into those reports, or else he'd been there that night to take the necklace while he'd murdered her mother.

Ivy had to close her eyes a moment to shut out the images. She'd been the one to discover her parents and had actually stepped in her mother's blood when she ran to the bodies. There'd been nothing she could do, and she didn't even remember making the frantic call to Gabriel. Good thing she had, too, because when he'd run to their parents', he'd discovered Jodi on the path. She was within minutes of bleeding out, and he'd managed to save her.

Something Ivy hadn't been able to do for her folks.

There were times, like now, when she reminded herself that the horror that'd gone on that night could have been even worse. Jodi could be dead, too. Maybe even Gabriel as well, since Jodi's attacker was probably nearby when her brother had found her. Remembering that soothed Ivy a little. But not enough to make the ache fade in her heart.

Theo finished the call he'd just made to the crime lab, glanced at her and frowned. "You can't dwell on it," he said.

It was as if he'd looked right into her mind—something he'd always had a knack for doing—but she didn't care much for it now. In some ways it made it worse that he knew how much she was still hurting. In some ways, though, it made it better. This wasn't a case of misery loving company, it was just that Theo understood how much she'd lost that night. Because he'd lost so much himself.

"How do you forget?" she asked. "How do you push it all aside?"

He stared at her, shook his head. "You don't." On a heavy sigh, he went to Gabriel's fridge, grabbed a bottle of water and brought it to her. "There's no permanent fix for grief. It keeps coming back."

Yes, it did. Like now. It was washing over her.

"Sometimes, it helps if I think about the good stuff," he added. He pushed her hair from her face, his fingers lingering on her cheek. "How close Jodi and I once were. The times I was with you. I just force myself to remember that there were more good times than bad."

Good advice. Too bad she couldn't take it. It was impossible to push away the fear. Or so she thought. But then she looked at Theo, their gazes connecting, and just like that, things were a little better.

And worse.

Because even now with all the bad memories flooding her mind, she noticed him. That rumpled hair. That mouth. Mercy, he had a way of getting right past the fear and into places inside her where he shouldn't be. Like her heart. Of course, her heart wasn't the only problem at the moment. Theo also knew how to stir up things in her body.

Yes, there'd been plenty of good times, and most of those moments had centered on him.

"I would ask you to go to the break room…" he said, arching his eyebrow as if that were a question rather than an attempt at a joke.

Despite everything going on, Ivy had to fight back a smile. "Probably not a good idea."

Theo kept his eyes on her as if waiting for something more. Conversation, maybe? An assurance that she was okay?

Another kiss?

If it was the kiss, then Ivy imagined it would be the kiss that people gave each other when they were used to kissing. When that kiss would suddenly make all the bad things go away. Something that it couldn't do. But it could cause the old heat to slide right through her. In fact, just the thought of kissing him did that to her. It also helped that Theo was so close to her that she caught his scent.

More of that heat came.

"I've seen that look before." He brushed his

fingers over the center of her forehead, which was bunched up.

Now she waited, because she wasn't sure where he was going with this. Maybe he had noticed the need in her expression. Or perhaps he was picking up on all the other things—the worry, the fatigue and, yes, the fear.

He didn't take his fingers from her face. Instead, Theo slipped them lower, to her cheek, and his touch—warm and soothing—lingered a moment there. Even though he didn't say anything, they had an entire conversation. About this mutual attraction that was messing with their minds. About what had torn them apart in the past. Even what might bring them back together in the future.

Nathan.

Theo must have realized this wasn't going to be something they could hash out now. Nor should they be doing this. Not with the danger still out there. And that's probably why he stepped back. Not far enough, though. Of course, several rooms over might not have been far enough to get her body to cool down.

"I'm sorry," he said, the frown returning.

Those two words certainly started the cooling-down process. "For what?"

"For not being able to keep you safe."

That's where she thought this was leading, and she didn't like it one bit. "I could be the reason you're in danger," she reminded him. Ivy was about to repeat his apology to him, but then she stopped when an idea went through her head. "Has anyone checked to see if my father was maybe investigating Wesley?"

She expected Theo to look surprised at the abrupt change in conversation, but he merely nodded. "I did last night. All your father's cases aren't digitized, but Gabriel did a summary of each of them and put the info in a master file and shared it with me."

Now Ivy was the one who was surprised, and she felt her eyes widen. She hadn't known about the master file or the sharing part, and Gabriel must have been able to get over the rocky past with Theo for him to give him that info.

"And?" she asked.

"Your father didn't specifically mention Wesley's name, but he was working on a case that involved SAPD. Sherman had busted some guys for drugs, and he found some guns on them that had been confiscated in a raid in San Antonio. The weapons had been reported as destroyed, but clearly they weren't."

Ivy took a moment to think that through. "So a San Antonio cop sold or gave them the gun?"

Theo lifted his shoulder. "Or it could have been a paperwork error. It happens," he added. "I'll keep digging, but so far I haven't found anything that connects Wesley to the chain of custody of those guns."

And without that, it would be almost impossible to tie Wesley to it—and to her father's murder.

Ivy shook her head. "Maybe I'm overthinking this. Your father was convicted of the murders, and he has never denied doing it." Of course, that was mainly because Travis had been drunk and couldn't remember. "Anyway, maybe Wesley isn't dirty at all. Maybe that drug bust my father made is just muddying already muddy waters."

Theo certainly didn't argue with that. Which meant they were back to Lacey and August. And speaking of August, Ivy heard the man's voice in the squad room. A very unhappy voice. It wasn't a shock that he was riled about being brought back in again for questioning.

"There'd better be a damn good reason you dragged me back here," August shouted. And yes, it was a shout. "Because I'm sick and tired of being accused of things I didn't do."

Gabriel had been at one of the deputies' desks, but he got to his feet and motioned for August to follow him. Her brother didn't shout, but he was scowling.

Both Theo and she stepped to the side so that Gabriel could lead August into his office. The watch, envelope and report were no longer there. They'd been couriered to the crime lab.

"First things first," Gabriel said to August. "Tell me about Belinda Travers."

"Who?" August made a face. "Never heard of her."

"Well, she's heard of you. She says you were supposed to meet her in a bar in San Antonio, but then someone kidnapped her."

"What?" August howled. "She's lying."

Gabriel and Theo exchanged glances, both of them clearly not happy with that denial. Maybe when the woman was able to talk to them, she could prove that August was the liar.

Gabriel dragged in a long breath and turned his computer monitor in August's direction. "Tell me about this," Gabriel ordered him. It was a picture of her father's watch.

Before August's attention actually landed

on the screen, he'd already opened his mouth. No doubt to shout something again about how innocent he was. But he not only closed his mouth, he also moved in closer for a better look.

"Where did you get that?" August demanded.

"I asked you a question first," Gabriel fired back. He didn't add more, maybe because he wanted to see where August would go with this.

It didn't take long for August to respond. He cursed. It wasn't exactly angry cursing, though. His shoulders dropped, and while he shook his head, August sank down on the edge of Gabriel's desk.

"Hell," August mumbled. That definitely wasn't a denial, and neither was his body language. "I need to know where you got the watch," August said, and this time it wasn't a demand. Even though he didn't add a *please*, it was there, unspoken.

"I figured it'd come from you," Gabriel answered.

Since August was a hothead, his normal response would have been to verbally blast Gabriel for suggesting that. He didn't. Mercy, did that mean it'd actually come from August? If so, how had he gotten it, and why had he used it to try to set up Lacey?

"Start talking," Theo ordered him. He stepped closer to his uncle, violating his personal space, and August spared him a glance before his gaze darted away.

"I found the watch shortly after Travis's trial," August explained after a long pause. "It was in the barn at Travis's ranch." He looked up at Theo. "You know that corner where your daddy used to store sacks of feed? Well, there were some loose boards on the wall," he said when Theo nodded. "I looked behind them and saw the watch."

Theo tilted his head, his mouth tightening. Gabriel had a similar expression—one of skepticism.

"SAPD went through that barn," Theo reminded him. "So did Gabriel and Jameson."

August nodded. "So did I, and I didn't see it. Someone had tucked it up behind the boards. I think the only reason I found it was that some of the nails had given way and caused the board to come loose."

Ivy supposed it was possible that Travis had taken the watch and then hidden it there. Well, it was believable if you discounted the fact that Travis had been drunk the night of the murders. Apparently, he'd been so drunk that he'd passed out shortly thereafter.

"How do you think my dad's watch got there?" Ivy came out and asked.

"I have no idea." Now August shifted his attention to her. "But this still doesn't make my brother guilty. The killer could have easily planted it there hours and even days after the crime. Like I said, I didn't find it until after the trial, and that was months later."

"You found it and yet you didn't turn it over to Gabriel?" Theo's mouth was in a flat line now.

"I couldn't see the point of it," August answered without hesitation. "Travis had just gotten a life sentence. I didn't think it would do much good if folks knew a dead man's watch had been found in his alleged killer's barn."

"It wasn't alleged," Gabriel said. "He was convicted. And you should have given the watch to me instead of trying to use it as some kind of ploy to set up Lacey Vogel."

"What?" August jumped to his feet, and she saw that flash of temper that'd been missing the last couple of minutes. "Is that what she said I did? Because I sure as hell didn't."

Theo and Gabriel exchanged more glances. Confused ones. Ivy was right there with them.

"Someone put the watch on Lacey's vehicle," Theo explained. "She tossed the watch aside, and that person then took it and sent it to a lab. It has both Sherman Beckett's blood and Lacey's prints. Not your prints, though. Why is that if you're the one who found it?"

August's gaze slashed between the two lawmen, and his eyes widened before he cursed again. "My prints weren't on it because I used a paper towel to pick it up. I then wrapped it in that towel and put it in Travis's house. In plain view on the coffee table in the living room. I figured if Jodi and Theo came back, they'd see it and turn it in."

Theo huffed. "Why the hell would you do that?"

Ivy wanted to know the same thing. To the best of her knowledge, Theo and Jodi had never gone back to the house. Like her own parents' house, Travis's place had been empty. Abandoned.

"I didn't want the watch at my house," August said as if that explained everything. "I just figured it'd be better if I left it at Travis's."

"Better because it would seem as if someone had put it there to taunt the police," Theo snapped. "You did that to try to make my father look innocent. Or at least that's why you did if you're telling us the truth."

"I am," August insisted.

Maybe he was, but if so, he didn't deny Theo's accusation about leaving the watch to make Travis appear innocent.

"Someone must have taken the watch from Travis's house," August went on. "But why would that person then want to set up Ivy's stepdaughter?"

Ivy didn't know, but she had a theory. "Lacey hates me and would do anything to get back at me. It wouldn't surprise me if she had had someone go through both my parents' and Travis's places. Maybe so she could find something she could use against me. Something to help her win a lawsuit to get her hands on her dad's money."

All three men were staring at her now. Maybe waiting for her to come up with more, but Ivy didn't have more. She didn't have a clue how Lacey would hope to connect the watch to her.

But Theo apparently did.

Still, there was something about all of this that didn't make sense. Ivy gave that some more thought but had to shake her head. "That seems like a lot of trouble to go through just to cast some doubt on my name."

Theo lifted his shoulder. "Maybe it's all she could find and figured she'd use it. By having her own prints on it, too, she might think it takes suspicion off her. It doesn't." Theo shifted his gaze to August. "Nor you. Gabriel could file charges against you for withholding evidence."

August's mouth practically dropped open, and he snapped to Gabriel. "By the time I found the watch, the investigation and the trial were over."

"Doesn't matter," Gabriel answered. "Anything connected to the case should have been given to me."

"What the hell would you have to gain by bringing charges against me?" August's temper was not only back, but it had also risen a couple of notches.

"Justice," Gabriel answered without hesitation. "Plus, if you'd given me the watch, we'd wouldn't be in this situation now of wondering who's trying to use it and why."

August would have no doubt responded to that with a fury-laced tirade, but Theo's phone rang, the sound knifing through the room. The moment Theo glanced at the screen, Ivy knew from his suddenly tight expression that there was a problem.

"It's Jameson," Theo told her, and he answered the call.

Ivy moved even closer to Theo so she could hear what her brother was saying, but it was a very short conversation. One that ended with Theo cursing and taking hold of her arm.

"We need to leave now," Theo said. "Jameson said there's an armed intruder on the grounds of the safe house."

Chapter Twelve

Theo had been on plenty of assignments where he'd faced down killers, but that suddenly felt like a drop in the bucket compared to what he was facing now.

His son could be in grave danger.

That in itself was bad enough, but in the back of his mind he also had to wonder if this was a trap to draw Ivy and him out for yet another attack. Hell, even that wasn't worse than an intruder going after Nathan.

"Just stay calm," Jodi said from the other end of the line.

She was whispering, something she'd done since she had taken over the call from Jameson. His sister was in the bathroom with Nathan while Jameson was at the front of the house to make sure the intruder they'd seen didn't get inside. She was keeping her voice low so that anyone outside the house wouldn't be able to hear her and pinpoint her location.

"Any idea where the intruder is now?" Gabriel asked from the front seat of the cruiser. He was driving—something he'd insisted on doing—not just so they'd have more backup but also because he'd been concerned that Theo and Ivy were too upset to be speeding down the rural road.

Gabriel was right. Theo was upset. But Ivy was to the point of being panicked. That was no doubt why Jodi kept reminding them to stay calm.

"Jameson just said he spotted the guy again," Jodi relayed. "He's in the ditch near the front of the road."

That probably meant the guy had tripped the motion sensor and that's how Jameson had known he was there in the first place. Maybe now that Jameson knew his location, he could just shoot him or keep him pinned down until they got there. Theo would have liked to have the guy alive, but he didn't want that to happen at the expense of Nathan, Jodi and Jameson.

"The ditch doesn't lead to the house," Jodi added. "Even if the man crawls toward us, the nearest he can get is about twenty yards."

That was still close. Too close. The goon could fire into the house, and the shots could make it through the walls and into the bathroom. Of course, if the gunman lifted his head to fire, Jameson should be able to take him out.

Provided the goon didn't shoot Jameson first, that is. But since that made Theo's own panic soar, he reminded himself that Jameson was a capable lawman. A lawman who was protecting his nephew and his brother's fiancée.

"How did this person find the safe house?" Ivy asked. Her voice was hoarse, no doubt because her throat was tight. Her knuckles were turning white from the grip she had on the seat. "Did he follow us the first time we went there?"

Not likely. Theo was almost certain they hadn't been followed, and it would have been fairly easy to spot someone doing that on this road.

"The listening device," Theo guessed. "Even though we whispered when we were inside, someone still could have heard us. Plus, all three of our suspects were in the sheriff's office and could have overheard something."

Ivy whispered the profanity that Theo was

thinking. They'd known about those possible bugs, but they'd gotten so caught up in the danger and investigation that they might not have been as careful as they could have been. Not just with the bug, either. Because it was also possible that someone had sneaked into the parking lot of the sheriff's building and planted tracking devices on the cruisers.

"Is Jameson sure there's just one intruder?" Ivy asked several moments later.

"He thinks just the one," Jodi answered.

His sister could be saying that to calm Ivy's nerves. But Theo figured the only thing that would calm her was for Ivy to see Nathan and make sure all was well. That might not happen for a while. For one thing, they were still a good ten minutes out. For another, the thug might start shooting at them the moment they got there. If he wasn't alone, then Gabriel could be driving right into a trap. That's the reason Theo took out his backup weapon and handed it to Ivy.

"It's just a precaution," he said when her eyes widened.

"Keep watch around us," Gabriel reminded them, and then added to Ivy, "That's a precaution, too."

A huge one. Because this stretch of road

had plenty of trees. Ditches, too. More thugs could be lying in wait for them.

Those last few miles seemed to take an eternity, though Theo was certain Gabriel was going as fast as he could safely go. When Gabriel finally reached the turn to the house, he slowed and glanced around.

"Jodi, I'm going to hang up and text Jameson," Gabriel told her. "I've got a visual on the house and the ditch, but I can't see the gunman." Gabriel did text his brother, and it only took a few seconds for Jameson to reply.

The guy is near the mailbox, Jameson responded, and Gabriel read the text to them.

"Get down on the seat," Theo instructed Ivy, and he lowered his window just a fraction. "If you drive up closer, I'll see if I can get this idiot to surrender," he added to Gabriel.

Gabriel did begin to inch the cruiser closer just as his phone buzzed with a call. "It's not Jameson," he said. "It's the hospital, but I'll call them back." Instead, he kept his attention on the ditch.

"Stand so we can see you," Theo called out to the man. "And put your hands in the air."

Theo figured there was no way that would work, and it didn't. Almost immediately, the man got to his feet. But he definitely did not put his hands in the air. Nor did he surrender. Instead he turned, aiming his gun at the cruiser, and he fired. The shot slammed into the front windshield. Just like the other attack, the glass held, but Theo couldn't risk this idiot firing shots that stood any chance whatsoever of hitting any of them.

"Stay down," Theo reminded Ivy, and he lowered the window even more. When the goon lifted himself to shoot at them again, Theo fired first.

His bullet hit the man squarely in the chest.

The goon fell backward, his weapon thudding to the ground next to him. Gabriel didn't waste any time driving the cruiser closer to him. Jameson came out the front of the house as well, but he stayed back on the porch. Probably because there could be other gunmen in the area.

Gabriel stopped the cruiser right next to the wounded man, and Theo opened his door wide enough to snatch up the thug's weapon. Of course, he could be carrying a backup, but at the moment he wasn't reaching for anything. He was clutching his chest.

And he was bleeding out.

Gabriel called for an ambulance, but Theo doubted it would get there in time. That meant anything they could get from the guy, he had to try to get it now.

"Who are you?" Theo demanded.

The guy shook his head. "My name won't mean anything to you."

"Try." Theo kept his gun pointed right at him.

"Morris Carlyn." He groaned in pain, pressing his hands even harder over his wound.

The name didn't mean anything to Theo, but it soon would. Gabriel fired off a text, no doubt to get a background on this guy. Once they had that, they might be able to link him to one of their suspects.

"Who sent you, Morris?" Theo asked.

Another headshake. "There's no threat you can make that'll be worse than what'll happen if I talk."

"Wanna bet?" Theo took aim at the guy's leg. "I can start putting bullets in you. It won't kill you any faster, but it'll make your last minutes on this earth very, very painful."

It was a bluff, of course. He couldn't shoot an unarmed, dying man, but mercy, that's what he wanted to do if it would help them put a stop to the danger.

The guy looked at him, their gazes connecting. "My family could be hurt. That's why I can't tell you. That's why I agreed to do this."

All right. So someone had maybe blackmailed or coerced him. Theo glanced at Gabriel to see if he was already on that. He was. Gabriel sent another text that probably included cops going to this guy's house to check on anyone who might be there.

"How did you find this place?" Theo continued.

"I was just told to come here and kidnap the woman, Ivy Beckett. I was supposed to take her alive."

Hell. That was hard to hear. Obviously hard for Ivy to hear, too, because she gasped.

If the guy was telling the truth, and that was still a big *if*, it didn't rule out any of their suspects. Wesley or Lacey would want Ivy alive so they could use her as a bargaining chip to get whatever it was they wanted. In Lacey's case so she could get the money. For Wesley, it could have been so he could maybe force Theo into a rescue situation so he could kill him. Because there was no way Theo wouldn't go after Ivy if this idiot had indeed managed to kidnap her.

It was ironic, though, that Wesley would be doing that because he thought Theo knew something about that botched militia raid. Other than a gut feeling, Theo had nothing, and you couldn't use gut feelings to make an arrest.

"Protect my family," the guy said, and his eyelids fluttered down. Dead, probably. But Theo wasn't about to get out and check on him.

Apparently, Gabriel wasn't, either, because he sped toward the house, and he pulled the cruiser to a stop directly in front of the porch. Ivy immediately bolted out, running past Jameson and going inside.

"Any sign of other gunmen?" Gabriel asked his brother as they rushed in behind Ivy.

"No. But the sensors are still working because they went off when you got here." Jameson armed the security system and then tipped his head to the ditch. "Is the guy dead?"

"Probably," Gabriel answered, and he went to the window to keep watch while he made a call. No doubt to follow up on the thug's family.

"Go ahead. Check on Nathan," Jameson told him when Theo kept looking in the direction of the hall bathroom. "Once we've regrouped and gotten more backup out here, we'll have to leave, though."

No way would Theo disagree with that. He wanted backup and plenty of it, but he also wanted Ivy and his son out of there. The location had been compromised, and that meant there could be another attack. Or another attempt to kidnap Ivy. Either way, they were all at risk.

The moment Theo stepped into the bathroom, Jodi hurried out, saying that she wanted to check on Gabriel. Theo stood there a moment and watched his sister go to the man she obviously loved. He saw the fear now, on her face and in her body language. The relief, too, that Gabriel was all right.

Theo felt that same relief when he looked at Nathan. Well, what he could see of him, anyway. Ivy had him wrapped in her arms, and even though she wasn't crying, she was blinking hard. No doubt to try to stave off the tears.

"Did you do something to the bad man?" Nathan asked him. He maneuvered himself back just enough so that he could make eye contact with Theo.

Theo nodded and hoped that would be enough of an explanation. He really didn't want to have to tell Nathan that he'd just killed someone.

"Does this mean we have to leave?" Nathan added.

"Yes," Ivy and Theo answered in unison.

Nathan didn't seem upset about that, but he did volley some glances at both Ivy and him. "Will you two get together?" he asked.

It was a repeat of the same question the boy had hit them with earlier. It was understandable for him to want to know. After all, whatever Ivy and he did would affect Nathan's future.

"I mean, since Mr. Chad is dead and you're my parents and all," Nathan added. "I just figured you'd get together."

Considering that Theo's mind was still whirling from the attack, it was hard to switch gears in the conversation. Especially when the switch was this big. Theo looked at Ivy to see if she had an idea of how to answer that.

She didn't.

The blank stare that she gave Theo let him know that.

"We'll talk about that soon," Theo settled for saying. "For now, why don't we go ahead and start gathering up your things so we'll be ready to leave when the other deputies get here?"

Nathan got moving right away, and Ivy and

Theo followed him to the bedroom not only to stand watch but to make sure he didn't go near the window. The blinds were down, curtains drawn, but there was no sense taking the risk.

"I can't go to the new safe house with him," Ivy said. Her voice was a hoarse whisper, and he saw that her hand was trembling when she touched her fingers to her mouth. "If someone is truly after me, I can't put him in danger like that."

Theo was already thinking along those same lines, but he doubted that Gabriel had two safe houses ready to go. That would take time.

Ivy turned to him, took hold of Theo's sleeve and pulled him out into the hall. "Just hear me out before you say no," she started.

And Theo groaned. Because he figured he wasn't going to like what would follow that comment.

"I think Jodi and Jameson should take Nathan to the backup safe house. Right away," Ivy added. "The deputies who are coming can follow them as backup. That'll get Nathan out of here in case there are other gunmen."

He couldn't object to any of that, but Theo could practically see where this was going.

"You're not going to make yourself bait," he insisted.

"Not bait." She glanced in at Nathan, then pulled Theo even farther away from the room before she repeated those two words. "But we can't let things continue like this. If whoever's behind this can't get to me, they might decide to go after Nathan."

Just the thought of it twisted his gut. So did the fact that Theo couldn't deny that. If this person became even more desperate, then things might escalate fast.

"You're still not making yourself bait," he warned her.

"Controlled bait," Ivy corrected, and she kept on talking despite Theo's protest. "While Nathan is safe with Jodi and Jameson—and you—Gabriel, Cameron and I can go back to Gabriel's place. We can use the ranch hands for extra protection. Maybe even set up some sensors like the ones that are here."

Theo was shaking his head before she even finished, but she took hold of his chin to stop him. "We can make things as safe as we can possibly make them," Ivy added.

That wasn't much of an argument, but then, no place was going to be completely safe. And yes, the ranch hands along with some motion detectors would beef up security. Maybe not enough, though.

"If we can sell Gabriel on this—and I'm not even sure I want to do that," Theo said, "then I wouldn't go with Nathan and the others. I'll be with you since the attack is most likely to happen at the ranch." Just saying that didn't help with the knot that was tightening even more in his stomach. "But first we need to find out if we can find the snake responsible for this before we have to do something this dangerous."

Ivy made a sound of agreement. "You mean talk to Belinda Travers. Gabriel got that call from the hospital, and it's probably about her. Maybe she's talking."

"Wait here with Nathan," Theo instructed, "and I'll find out."

Theo went back to the living room, where he found Jodi, Jameson and Gabriel all standing watch at the window. "Is Nathan okay?" Gabriel immediately asked him.

Theo nodded. "Ivy wants to send him to a separate safe house."

Even though Theo didn't explain Ivy's "controlled bait" idea, Gabriel obviously filled in the blanks because his mouth tightened. What he didn't do was dismiss it.

And that caused Theo to curse. "Belinda's not talking?"

Gabriel gave a heavy sigh. "She's dead."

Hell. Well, there went the notion of questioning her, but it was more than that. From the looks of things, Belinda had been innocent in all of this, and someone had murdered her. That someone wanted to do the same to Ivy, too.

"Please tell me someone didn't sneak into the hospital and finish her off," Theo said.

"No. She developed a blood clot. The doc told me that sometimes things like that happen."

Yeah. Bad things happened all the time. Theo had to make sure now that the bad things didn't continue with Nathan and Ivy.

"I think it's too late for the guy in the ditch, but just in case, the ambulance is on the way," Gabriel continued while he volleyed glances between Theo and the window. "The deputies will be here soon, too."

"What about the guy's family?" Theo wanted to know. "Any idea if they're really in danger?"

"I called SAPD as soon as we were all back in the house," Jameson volunteered. "They're on the way to check on them."

Theo hoped they were all right, but after

what had happened to Belinda, it was possible the man's family was also in danger.

"Is there another safe house?" Theo's question got all of their attention. Ivy's as well, since she was now in the hall with Nathan behind her.

"One that's ready now," Gabriel answered. "It'll take me a while to set up another one."

"Wait in your room for just a few more minutes," Ivy told Nathan.

Judging from his pinched expression, that was the last thing Nathan wanted to do. The kid was no dummy, and he must have known that something big was about to happen. Still, he went into his room, and Ivy came closer to them. That's when Theo saw that she was blinking back tears again.

"Look, I don't want to be away from my son. Nor do I want to die." Ivy's voice was shaking, and one of those tears made it down her cheek. She quickly wiped it away.

Theo went to her and slid his arm around her waist. He doubted it would help. Nothing much would at this point.

"We have to put an end to this—*now*," Ivy insisted. "That means using me to draw out this monster."

Since Theo had already voiced his opinion

on this, he stayed quiet and waited for Gabriel to tell her no way in hell was he going to put his sister in danger like that. But Gabriel didn't get a chance to say anything because Jameson's phone buzzed.

"It's SAPD," Jameson said. He answered the call but didn't put it on speaker. Several moments later, he cursed. "The gunman's house has been ransacked, and his wife and two kids are missing." Jameson paused, his attention going to Ivy. "Someone left a note on the guy's door."

"A note about me?" Ivy asked. Theo felt the muscles in her body tense.

Jameson nodded. "The note said, and I'm quoting, 'Tell Theo that Ivy will be next. She dies tonight.'"

Chapter Thirteen

The note had chilled Ivy to the bone. It still did even several hours later. But it had been the final straw needed to convince Theo and her brothers that the only way to end this was to draw out the killer.

Not just for their sakes but for the gunman's family, too.

Ivy now knew that Morris Carlyn's family had indeed been kidnapped, and the cops didn't think it was a staged crime scene, either. The person who'd hired Morris had likely taken them to get him to cooperate. If he'd lived, that is. He hadn't, and Ivy prayed that meant the family would be released soon. While she was praying, she added several for Nathan and the rest of them.

She dies tonight.

If that was true, then she only had five or

six hours before this monster tried to come after her. Five or six hours to get everything in place so that at least Nathan would be safe.

"It's time to go," Gabriel said as he disarmed the security system.

That was Ivy's cue to give Nathan one last hug and kiss before he went off with Jameson, Cameron and Jodi. Ivy trusted all three of them to keep her boy safe, but even though she seemed to be the target, there were no guarantees the culprit might not try to use Nathan the way he or she had used Morris's family.

"It'll be okay?" Nathan asked, but it took Ivy a moment to realize he'd aimed that question at Theo. "You'll take care of my mom?"

Theo certainly wasn't the ice man–lawman right now. His eyebrows were drawn together, and muscles in his shoulders looked stiff. "I will."

Nathan seemed to accept that because he nodded, went to Theo and hugged him. Everyone in the room looked surprised. Especially Theo. He hesitated just a moment before his arms went around Nathan to return the hug.

Ivy had been near tears all day, and seeing that put some fresh ones in her eyes. Over the years she hadn't allowed herself to consider how Theo would be with Nathan, but she could see how much he loved their son.

Theo brushed a kiss on top of Nathan's head, and the boy pulled back, meeting his gaze. "Will you teach me to ride a bull? Because Aunt Jodi said you used to ride them and that you were good at it."

Theo shot his sister a "thanks for nothing" glance. "Maybe when you're a little older," he answered.

Again, Nathan seemed to accept that because he smiled, gave Theo another hug and then hurried to the door next to Gabriel. "I know," Nathan said to him. "We gotta run fast when we get outside."

Since every one of them had mentioned that in some way or another, Ivy was glad it had sunk in. She went to the door, too, and from the side window, she saw that Cameron had pulled an unmarked police car next to the porch. Earlier, he'd gotten Nathan's things and put them in the trunk, and he'd already opened the back passenger's door.

Jodi and Jameson didn't waste any time getting Nathan outside and into the vehicle. Cameron immediately sped away. A second car with two reserve deputies followed them for backup.

"The new safe house is about ten miles from here," Gabriel said, "but it'll be a while before they get there."

Yes, because Cameron would have to drive around to make sure they weren't being followed. Gabriel had already explained that to her along with the assurance that all the vehicles had been checked and double-checked for bugs and tracking devices. Gabriel and the others had made it as safe as they possibly could, considering that Nathan would essentially be out in the open.

"Now it's our turn," Gabriel instructed.

Another of the deputies, Edwin Clary, pulled a cruiser in front of the house. This one was definitely marked with Blue River Sheriff emblazoned on the side, as was the one behind them that Deputy Jace Morrelli was driving. Along with Gabriel and Theo, that meant there'd be four lawmen driving her back to the ranch.

As Nathan and the others had done, they hurried to get into the cruiser, and Edwin drove them away. Ivy ended up in the middle of the back seat between Gabriel and Theo, and she automatically sank lower since she figured one of them would soon tell her to do that. However, she kept her head just high enough to help them keep watch.

"We're going straight to the ranch," Gabriel continued, "even if someone follows us."

Ivy had figured that's how things would be, but it still sent a chill through her to hear it aloud.

"What's the plan once we're there?" Edwin asked. The deputy made eye contact in the mirror with Gabriel as he turned onto the road that would take them back to the ranch.

"The hands know we're coming, and they're all armed. Not out in the pastures, though. They've been setting up some sensors and cameras they got from the office to set up motion detectors and surveillance spots on the paths that lead to the house. Once they're finished, I want them out of sight."

It was smart to set up the equipment. Because the road was highly visible from Gabriel's house, but there were two paths that someone could use to get to them. In fact, the man who'd attacked Jodi ten years ago had used one of them. Maybe Travis had as well the night he'd murdered her parents. Those paths were lined with bushes and trees—the perfect place for a person to hide.

"Whoever comes after you," Gabriel continued, "we need to take him or her alive. That's the only way we're going to be able to figure out who's behind this."

Yes, especially considering that Belinda and Morris were dead and Morris's family was missing.

"That's why I want the hands and all of us tucked away. I don't want whoever's coming to see too many guns and turn back."

In other words, Gabriel was going to make it look like it would be an easy attack. Of course, the person behind this likely knew that it wouldn't be and would probably bring lots of firepower.

Ivy looked up at Theo the moment he looked down at her, and she saw something in his eyes that she was certain was in her own. A parent's worry. This was still a fairly new feeling for Theo, and she wished she could tell him that it would go away. It didn't. Even when there wasn't this kind of danger looming over them, she always worried about Nathan.

"Don't worry," Theo said. "I won't teach him how to ride a bull. Not anytime soon, anyway." The corner of his mouth lifted for just a moment.

Ivy was glad at his attempted humor. Glad, too, that it eased her racing heart just a little.

She wanted to tell him she was glad he was there, but because he was there, with her, he was also at risk of being killed.

"How does Nathan do in school?" Theo asked. He glanced away from her to keep watch.

It seemed like such a, well, normal conversation. Definitely not the gloom and doom they'd been discussing since his return to Blue River.

"He gets As and Bs," she answered. "He struggles some with math, but he's way ahead in reading. In sports, too. He loves playing baseball."

Ivy realized she, too, was smiling a little, and she understood that's why Theo had talked about Nathan in the first place. That was probably the only thing that could help with the nerves. For a few seconds, anyway. And then Ivy felt the blasted tears threaten again.

On a heavy sigh, Theo slid his arm around her. She had on her seat belt, but Theo didn't, and he eased across the seat toward her. As he'd done with Nathan, he brushed a kiss on the top of her head.

"Thank you," she whispered. She automatically slid into the crook of his arm.

"Don't thank me yet," he whispered back, and she got the feeling they were talking about more than just the danger yet to come.

She looked up at him and got confirmation of that. The heat was still there. Simmering. And the kisses in Gabriel's office hadn't done a thing to cool it down. However, what did help was when Gabriel's phone buzzed, because that quickly got her attention. Theo's, too, since he moved back across the seat.

"It's nothing to do with Nathan," Gabriel said right off. "It's one of the hands. They have everything in place, and they're moving to their hidden positions now."

Good. Because they weren't far from the ranch now. Only a couple of minutes out.

"When we get there," Gabriel went on, looking at her, "I'll have Edwin pull up in front of the porch, and Theo, you and I will go inside. Edwin will leave and drive back toward town, but he'll actually pull off on a trail not far from here so he can make a quick response if necessary."

Ivy hoped it would be quick enough.

"I want you and Theo to go upstairs to the guest bathroom," Gabriel continued. "The hands have put a laptop there so you can watch the security cameras."

It took Ivy a moment to process that, and she didn't like where this was going. "If an attack happens, it'll likely be on the ground level of the house—where you'll be."

Gabriel nodded. "And I'll know they're coming before they even get here. I don't want to make this easy for whoever's after you by giving someone the opportunity to just start firing shots into the place. There's also another cruiser parked out of sight in the barn, and if things get bad, I want Theo to get you there and drive the two of you off the ranch. Don't worry, the hands and I will get out, too."

That caused every muscle in Ivy's body to tense. She didn't want her brother or anyone else right in the line of fire, but that might happen no matter where they were on the grounds. The trick would be to spot a possible attacker and capture him before he could even pull the trigger.

"The hands have made sure someone's not already on the grounds?" Theo asked.

"As much as humanly possible. They've been looking around since I called them a couple of hours ago."

But the hands could have missed a gunman who was hiding. The ranch was huge, and there were a lot of places for someone to stay out of sight of the hands.

"Hell," Gabriel grumbled.

Theo cursed, too, and Ivy lifted her head even higher to see what had caused their reactions. She soon saw the cause. There was a car parked just off the road where they were to take the final turn to the ranch.

And Wesley was there, leaning against the car as if waiting for them.

It wasn't an ideal spot for an ambush since there were no trees nearby, but that didn't mean Wesley didn't have something up his sleeve.

"What the heck does he want?" Theo added under his breath. His gun was already drawn, but he turned it in Wesley's direction.

"Should I stop?" Edwin asked.

The muscles in Theo's face tightened. "Yeah. Stop right here."

They were still a good twenty yards from Wesley, and Theo took out his phone. Since Ivy was sitting right next to him, she saw when he pressed Wesley's number, and when the man answered.

"I'm not going to shoot you," Wesley snarled. "You can come closer."

"This is close enough," Theo snarled right

back, and he put the call on speaker. "Why are you here?"

She had no idea how long Wesley had been there, and since he was a good half mile from the ranch, the hands probably had no idea he was there. Still, for someone who'd come out this way to see them, he didn't jump to answer Theo's question.

However, Wesley did mutter some profanity that she could still hear from the other end of the phone line. "I came to apologize. I was wrong to accuse you of anything criminal."

"You were wrong, but you didn't have to come out here to tell me that. How'd you even know I'd be here?"

Wesley lifted his shoulder. "I went by the sheriff's office, but no one would tell me where you were. I wanted to talk to you face-to-face, and figured sooner or later Ivy would want to come home. And that you'd be the one to bring her."

To most people that probably wouldn't have sounded like a threat, but it did coming from this man. Of course, that probably had something to do with the fact that he was still a suspect.

"I didn't have anything to do with what

went wrong with that raid," Wesley went on. "It's important you know that."

"Why?" Theo didn't ease up on the intensity in his voice. Nor his expression, either.

Wesley cursed again, and looked away. "I don't want anybody watching my every move. I don't want people to think I'm a dirty agent."

"Too late. They already think that." Theo paused a heartbeat while he kept watch around them. Edwin and Gabriel did the same. "Let me guess—Dwight Emory has started some kind of internal affairs investigation on you?"

Bingo. Even though Wesley didn't confirm that, Ivy could see enough of his face to know that it was not only true but that Wesley was riled about it. He certainly wasn't looking apologetic now.

"I won't let this ruin my career," Wesley spat out. "Or my life," he corrected. "Just know that I expect you to stop it. You need to tell Emory I did nothing wrong."

Ivy figured there was little or no chance of that happening, which made her wonder why Wesley had really come. Was it to find out if they were at the ranch? If so, he now knew they were, and if he was the person after them, they might not have to wait long for this to all come to a head.

"Drive," Theo instructed Edwin. "We've wasted enough time here." And with that, he hit the end call button but not before Ivy heard Wesley curse some more. The man continued to curse, too, when Edwin sped past him.

Ivy braced herself in case Wesley took out his gun and fired at them. But he didn't. She watched as he got back in his car, and he drove away—in the opposite direction of the ranch. Of course, that didn't mean he wouldn't just double back.

"What the hell was that all about?" Gabriel grumbled.

Theo shook his head. "I figure Emory put him on suspension, pending an internal affairs investigation."

An investigation that could be connected to the attacks against them if Wesley was indeed trying to silence Theo. Maybe Emory could find something against Wesley before things went from bad to worse.

Edwin took the turn to the ranch and drove through the cattle gate. She didn't see any hands, cameras or sensors, but Ivy figured they were all there. Another thing that wasn't in sight was the wedding decorations that had been on the fences. Someone had taken down the blue bows, a reminder that Gabriel's and

Jodi's lives had been thrown into chaos, as well. They should be on their honeymoon by now, and here Gabriel was, preparing to face down a killer.

A ranch hand stood in the opened doorway of Gabriel's house, and the moment Edwin stopped the cruiser, Gabriel, Theo and she rushed inside. Gabriel set the security system.

"It won't be dark for a while," Gabriel reminded them, "but I don't want you two out of the bathroom. If you need something, call me, and I'll bring it to you," he added. "Oh, and you can use the laptops to monitor the security cameras. The motion detectors shouldn't pick up slight movement like a small animal or such, but if you hear a beep, it means we've got someone where they shouldn't be."

Someone who would almost certainly be there to kill them.

Theo and she didn't waste even a second. They went upstairs to the guest bath suite, and they locked the door just in case someone managed to break in.

"Don't turn on the lights." Theo put his hand over hers when she automatically reached for the switch. Both his touch and the warning caused her to look at him. The warning because it was a reminder that they could still be targets here. The touch, well, because even something that simple could cause a swirl of heat to go through her body.

Of course, the timing sucked for that, so Ivy stepped away. It wasn't a tiny space, not with the private toilet area, bathtub and massive walk-in closet all in separate rooms. But she suspected it wasn't the large space that had caused her brother to want them there. It was the natural stone walls in the shower. Like the cruisers, it would be bullet-resistant.

Ivy had been using this bathroom and adjacent bedroom during her stay at the ranch, but someone had added a few things. There was bottled water, a gun with extra ammo, some snacks and a laptop—which Theo went to right away. He sank down on the floor with the computer and booted it up.

"Stay away from the window," Theo added.

She did, though it was impossible to see in or out of it since it was made of glass blocks. Still, it wouldn't stop bullets like the stone.

Ivy watched the laptop, and it didn't take long for the images from the security cameras to appear on the screen. Six total. And while the cameras covered the ranch grounds, that still didn't mean someone couldn't snake their way through the trees and shrubs, staying out of sight of both the cameras and the hands. Though if that happened, maybe the motion sensors would detect them.

"I used to sneak to your old house this way," Theo said. He tapped the screen to the right of her parents' house. No one lived there now, but once there'd been a trail of sorts that led from the road and then coiled around to the back of the place where Ivy met him at the back door and let him in.

"Sneaked him in" was closer to the truth. Her parents had never been keen on her seeing Theo, so to avoid the arguments with them, it was just easier to let them believe she wasn't seeing him.

"I remember. My bedroom was on that side of the house, and sometimes I'd sit in the window and watch for you when you were coming over."

Actually, she'd done that even when he hadn't said he would be over. Theo had pretty much dominated her thoughts in those days.

In some ways, he still did.

Like now, for instance.

His attention was on the laptop, but in profile she could still see enough of his face to bring back the old memories. Of their first kiss. The first time they'd made love. Ivy had been a virgin—Theo hadn't been—but it had felt incredibly special. Like something that'd never happened between two people before.

She silently cursed just how naive she'd been in those days. Because many couples probably felt that way. Couples who had managed to stay together and not be ripped apart by something as tragic as murder.

Theo went to another screen, this one on the trail that led from the old house to Gabriel's. Something caught her eye, and it must have caught Theo's as well because he zoomed in on a spot on the ground. She sank down on the floor next to him, their backs against the vanity while he made the necessary keystrokes to get the right angle.

Ivy hadn't realized she'd been holding her breath until she got a closer look and then relaxed. "It's one of the blue bows that'd been on the fences. A wedding decoration," she added. "It must have blown off and landed there."

Theo made a sound of agreement but zoomed in even more. Maybe to make sure the bow wasn't covering something like a weapon. But it wasn't. They were able to determine that when the wind blew it again and it skittered against one of the shrubs.

"Blue, Jodi's favorite color," Theo remarked.

"She used to plan her wedding to Gabriel when she was just a kid. She had a notebook with pictures she'd cut out of magazines."

Ivy nodded. "I remember. I also remember Gabriel always saying he was too old for her."

"At the time, he was. Five years is a big gap when she was just thirteen, and he was already legally an adult."

Yes. But that hadn't stopped Jodi from making those plans or her feelings for Gabriel. Now, here all this time later, she would finally get to marry the man she'd dreamed about, the man she loved.

"I used to plan our wedding," Ivy mumbled. Oh, mercy. She hadn't meant to say that aloud, so she quickly added, "You know, when I was a kid."

Actually, she'd been a teenager and was still planning it right up to the time of the big blowup and murders.

Theo turned to her, and she got a much better look at his face now that it wasn't just his profile. And she felt that old punch of heat. Definitely not a good time for it, so she looked away.

Theo didn't, though.

From the corner of her eye she could see he was still watching her. Probably because he was stunned by what she'd just said. As a teenage boy, he certainly wouldn't have been into wedding planning and such.

"Did you ever hate me for leaving?" he asked.

Now she was the one who was stunned. "No." It probably would have been a good time for her to at least pause and pretend to think about that. A good time, too, for there not to be so much heat in her voice. It was probably in her eyes, too. They'd been skirting this attraction since they'd come back to Blue River, but the skirting stopped suddenly.

Theo slid his hand around the back of her neck, pulled her to him and kissed her.

THIS KISS HAD *mistake* written all over it. And worse, Theo had known he was going to kiss Ivy from the moment she sat on the floor next to him. He also had known it would be good.

It was.

But that still didn't mean they should be doing this. For one thing, it was the quickest way for him to lose focus. Of course, Theo's body had a comeback for that—at the moment, there was no danger, and if that changed, the sensors would alert them to it. Still, this wasn't the right time or the right place. Too bad the thing that overrode that solid argument was that while everything else about it was wrong, Ivy was the right woman.

She always had been, and even though it'd been ten years since they'd been together, it was as if all those years vanished. All the old baggage, too. A good kiss could do that.

Along with making him stupid.

Theo should just end the kiss, move away from her and go back to watching the computer screen. But he didn't. Not only did he keep things at the stupid level by continuing the making out, he upped the ante by deepening the kiss and pulling Ivy even closer to him.

Ivy didn't exactly shy away from this, either. In fact, she was the one who moved the laptop to the counter so that there was nothing in between them. No reason for them not to position themselves so that his chest ended up against her breasts.

Theo kept kissing her, too. Kept moving her until she was practically in his lap. All in all, it was a good place for her to be if they were going to have sex, but he was pretty sure that shouldn't happen. Of course, he felt the same way about the kiss, but that hadn't stopped him.

Ivy finally stopped, though. She took her mouth from his, eased back and met him eye to eye. He figured she was about to apologize or say something else before she moved back to the floor.

She didn't.

"Don't overthink this," she said.

Since that's exactly what he was doing, Theo hesitated and stared at her. Along with the old baggage vanishing, so did the years. Suddenly, he was nineteen again and wanting Ivy more than his next breath. He hadn't had much willpower, but that ate up the rest of it.

Theo pulled her back to him and kissed her.

This time there was definitely no over-thinking. Hell, no thinking at all. He just kept kissing her until the fire was burning so hot inside him that he knew sex was going to happen even if it shouldn't.

Thankfully, Ivy was on the same page. Without breaking the kiss, she lowered her hands to his shirt and started to unbutton it. It was not a graceful effort. For one thing, Theo was trying to get her clothes off, too, and their hands kept bumping against each other. Still, he was finally successful at pulling off her top. He flung it to the side, and in the same motion, he turned Ivy and laid her back on the floor.

Because they'd been teenage lovers, they'd rarely had the luxury of a bed for sex. And Theo hated that they didn't have it now. Ivy darn sure deserved better than this, but there was no way he could risk taking her into the bedroom.

"Don't overthink this," she repeated.

She went after his shirt again, succeeded in getting it off him, and then she went after his jeans' zipper. Since things were moving fast, Theo got in some foreplay before the heat built to a point that they'd be beyond that. He took the kiss from her mouth to her neck. Then to her breasts. That brought back some sweet memories, and they got even sweeter when he unhooked her bra, bared her breasts and kissed her the way he wanted.

Ivy made a sound of pleasure and pulled him on top of her. Not a bad place to be, but he wasn't done yet. Theo went lower, dropping some kisses on her stomach while he unzipped her jeans and shimmied them off her.

Her panties went next.

And Theo probably would have kept kissing her for a few more seconds, but Ivy had a different notion about that. She latched onto him, hauling him back up to her so that she could kiss his mouth. And unzip him.

Theo didn't have much of a mind left. Not with his body burning to ash. But he did remember to take the condom from his wallet before Ivy got him out of his jeans. He also remembered how to put it on. No easy feat with Ivy still kissing him and trying to pull him into her.

The moment he had on the condom, he stopped resisting her attempts, and he slipped into her. Hell. He got another slam of memories. Of the first time they'd been together like this, and that slam only fired up his body even more. Definitely not something he needed, because this was already going to end much too fast. The pleasure was always too fast with Ivy, and like those other times, Theo tried to hold on to it.

She lifted her hips, bringing him even deeper into her, and Theo had no choice. There was no holding back, no more trying to draw this out to savor the pleasure. So he took control of the pace. As much as he could, anyway. He kept moving inside her. Kept holding her. Kept kissing her.

Until it was impossible to hold out any longer. Especially when Ivy came in a flash. She made that sound of pleasure again. Gathered him in her arms. And she gave Theo no choice. He let Ivy take him right along with her.

Chapter Fourteen

Ivy dressed while she waited for Theo to come out of the private bathroom area. She figured he wouldn't be in there long, which meant she needed to try to compose herself before she had to face him.

The sex had been amazing, and while that pleasure was still causing her body to hum, she doubted that Theo would be humming. No. He was probably already regretting this.

He would see it as a lapse in judgment, something that had caused him temporarily to lose focus. Heck, he might even regret it because it was too much, too soon between them. Either way, she didn't want to look as if she expected something more than sex between them.

Don't overthink this, she'd told him.

Well, it was advice she needed to take, as

well. What was done was done, and she'd just have to deal with the consequences later. In hindsight, though, Theo and she should have worked out a few things before having sex.

Ivy pushed all of that aside, put on her clothes and sat back on the floor with the laptop. There were still no signs of an intruder. Both a blessing and a curse. Part of her wanted this to come to a quick end so she could see Nathan. Another part of her wished there was a different way. One that didn't involve her brother and the hands in possible harm's way.

Theo's phone was still on the floor, and when it buzzed, she started to tell him he had a call. But then she saw Jameson's name on the screen and hit the answer button.

"Is Nathan okay?" she immediately asked.

Jameson hesitated a moment, maybe because he'd been expecting Theo to answer, and Theo must have heard the buzzing sound because he raced back into the main part of the bathroom. He was dressed for the most part but was still zipping up his jeans.

"He's fine," Jameson answered, and with a huge breath of relief leaving her mouth, she put the call on speaker and handed the phone to Theo. "We're all fine. Jodi and he are eating right now so I stepped into the bedroom to call you. I just got an update on Morris's family. I've already told Gabriel, but he said I should call you because he's basically got you and Theo locked in the bathroom...together," her brother added.

Even though Ivy couldn't see Jameson's face, he'd probably lifted an eyebrow over that. He knew that Theo and she couldn't keep their hands off each other. And they hadn't. But no way was she going to get into that.

"Did the cops find Morris's family?" Theo prompted when Jameson didn't continue.

"Yeah. They were in a motel just off the interstate. A maid found them. They were tied up, gagged and blindfolded but otherwise physically fine."

Ivy was betting that wasn't true of their mental state. Unless they were faking this, that is. "Who do they say took them?" Ivy asked.

"They don't know. The wife said that she and her daughter got back from shopping, and someone was in the house. The person used a stun gun on them. The guy carried them to a car and drove around with them for hours. In fact, he drove so long that he had to stop for gas."

"Certainly the thug made or got a call or two during that time," Theo pointed out.

"He made one call at the beginning of

the drive and told the person that he had the 'goods,'" Jameson answered. "Neither the wife nor the daughter could hear anything the caller said, but their kidnapper assured whoever it was that he would keep driving until he got further orders."

All of this had no doubt happened while Morris was on his way to the safe house to attack them.

"The kidnapper received a call right before he dropped them off at the motel," Jameson added. "By then, they must have known Morris had failed and there was no reason to hold his family."

Yes, and the kidnapper's boss could have already started lining up the next thug he or she could use to storm the ranch. Thank God the person had seen no value in killing Morris's family. Of course, there was another thing to consider. If Morris had voluntarily been in on this, then his family could have faked the kidnapping and release. They might not know the truth about that unless they caught the man or woman who was responsible.

"The guy who stun-gunned Morris's family wasn't wearing a mask?" Theo asked her brother.

"No. The wife was able to give a description of the man, but it's a pretty vague one. Not sure we'll actually get much from it."

Even if they did, the guy was probably long gone by now.

"I'll get in touch with you if anything else comes up," Jameson assured them, and he paused again. "I guess you two have plenty to talk over once we're out of this mess. Let me know if I can help with that." And he ended the call before Theo or she could even respond.

Theo put his phone in his pocket, and even though his attention went back to the laptop, Ivy knew he was thinking about what her brother had just said. She certainly was. But she didn't have time to dwell on it because there was a soft knock at the door.

"It's me," Gabriel said.

Since he could have critical information, Ivy hurried to let him in. Theo stood, too, but he volleyed his attention between Gabriel and the laptop. Gabriel's eyes did some volleying as well—between Theo and her.

"Is everything…okay?" Gabriel asked her.

She nodded and hoped it didn't look as if Theo and she had just had sex. But judging from her brother's huff, it did look that way.

"The last time Theo and you tangled, you

left town for ten years," Gabriel reminded her. "I'd rather that not happen again. In fact, when this danger is over and done, I want you to consider moving back here. It'd be a good place to raise Nathan."

It would be. Though she'd been comfortable enough at her own ranch, it had never quite felt like home.

"You wouldn't have to move in here," Gabriel added. He must have taken her silence to mean that she needed more convincing. "We could build you a place or you could have the old house."

"Definitely no to the old house. Too many bad memories there."

If she came back for good, Ivy would want a fresh start. Something that didn't add to the weight on her shoulders. Of course, that led her to the next thought that was on her mind.

Where did Theo fit in with this fresh start?

He'd said something about a desk job in San Antonio, but Ivy wasn't sure if he was certain of that or not. It was one thing to love his son and want to spend time with him, but it was another thing to completely alter his life.

"Is something wrong?" Theo asked, his attention on Gabriel now.

Because she'd been so caught up in the conversation, Ivy only then realized that Gabriel probably hadn't come up there to talk about their future. That sent her pulse racing, and it raced even more when Gabriel didn't jump to answer.

"Look at the camera that shows the old house," Gabriel instructed Theo. "You'll have to zoom in."

Ivy practically ran back to the laptop so she could see what was going on, but after frantically searching the screen, she had to shake her head. She didn't see anyone moving around or lurking in the shadows. But she did see an open window on the second floor.

"I'm pretty sure that window was closed last time I checked, and I didn't notice it until a few minutes ago."

It was open, not fully, though, only by a couple of inches. Since there were no lights on in the old house, it was just a gaping dark space. However, Ivy could see the reason for his concern—that window was lined up directly with Gabriel's house.

"The hands searched the place when we were on the way here," her brother continued, "but someone could have been hiding."

Yes, there was a huge attic along with enough

rooms and closets that the hands could have missed someone. Someone like a gunman.

"Have you seen any kind of movement in the window?" Theo asked without taking his attention off the screen.

"No. And I considered having a deputy and a couple of hands go down there to check it out, but I decided against it. Too risky at this point."

Definitely, because the deputy and hands would be out in the open and could be gunned down.

"Just keep a close watch on it," Gabriel told them. "I'll focus on the other cameras."

Good idea, because whoever had opened the window could have meant to do that as a distraction. Maybe to lure them out. Or maybe just to take their attention off another hiding place.

Gabriel started to leave, and Ivy followed so she could relock the door. But Theo said a single word of profanity that stopped them both. With Gabriel right behind her, Ivy went back so she could see for herself what had caused Theo's reaction.

And her heart went to her knees.

Because of what was now in the open window of the old house.

The barrel of a rifle.

FROM THE MOMENT they'd come back to the ranch, Theo had known an attack was possible. Likely, even. But it still gave him an adrenaline spike to see that weapon now pointed at Gabriel's house.

"Get in the shower now," Theo told Ivy.

Gabriel rushed out of the bathroom, no doubt so he could get to one of the windows downstairs so he'd be in position to return fire if it came down to that. Theo locked the door behind him and carried the laptop into the shower with Ivy and him, but not before Ivy grabbed a gun.

Her breathing was already way too fast, and Theo considered trying to do something to help her level it. But if he pulled her into his arms now, it would definitely be a distraction, and he needed to keep his attention on the rifle.

It was already dark, but there was enough of a moon to see the light glint off the barrel. Enough to see, too, when the barrel shifted just a little, and Theo spotted the scope on it. The shooter was taking aim at something, and he hoped it wasn't a ranch hand or deputy who wasn't hidden well enough.

"A shot from there would be able to make it here," she said.

It wasn't a question. She knew it could. But he hated to hear the slight tremble in her voice. Both of them wanted this showdown, but there was plenty of worry and fear, too.

Theo watched as the barrel shifted again, and he steeled himself for what he figured would come next. He didn't have to wait long.

The gunman fired.

Three shots, one right behind the other. Theo couldn't tell exactly where they'd landed, but they'd definitely hit Gabriel's house.

The shooter turned the barrel again, and the goon fired more shots. Not at the house this time. It didn't take Theo long to figure out what had been the gunman's new target.

One of the security cameras.

He'd shot out the one in Gabriel's backyard. That portion of the laptop screen went blank.

"The security system is still on," Theo reminded Ivy when she made a slight gasp. "If anyone tries to get into the house, the alarm will sound."

Plus, there were five other cameras and motion detectors. Theo figured, though, that the shooter would try to take out most of them.

And he did.

The next round of gunfire destroyed the

camera on the side of the house, the one that had allowed them to see the rifleman.

"He's setting up an attack," Ivy said, her voice a little shaky, but she kept a steady grip on the gun she was holding.

Theo hoped like the devil that she wouldn't have to use the weapon. While he was hoping, he added that maybe the ranch hands would spot this snake before he could get anywhere near Ivy.

They lost a third camera with the next shots. This one near the front porch, and it meant they now had a huge blind spot in the area that divided the two houses. Since that was also where the shooter was, Theo doubted that was a coincidence, and it meant the gunman would probably try to make his way to Gabriel's.

The silence came, and in many ways it was worse than the shots. As long as the guy was firing, Theo had known his location. Now he had no idea where the shooter was. However, he kept watch on the three other cameras since someone could be coming from that direction, too.

There was some movement on the screen from the camera on the other side of the house. Not an attacker. It was Al Talley, one of the ranch hands. He was at the back of a shed, and since Theo hadn't spotted him earlier, it meant Al had probably been in the shed itself. Maybe the gunfire had drawn him out.

Hell, or Al could have heard the sound of someone approaching.

Theo was about to text Gabriel to see if he knew what was going on, but the next shot stopped him cold. Because this one didn't go downstairs. It slammed into the window just a few feet from the shower. The bullet tore through the chunk of glass and sent it flying across the room.

"The shooter knows we're in here," Ivy whispered. Her grip tightened on the gun. She made a strangled sound of fear that came from deep within her chest.

Yeah, he did. That probably meant he was using some kind of thermal scanning equipment that could pinpoint them. The next shot proved it, too, because it tore through another chunk in the window, and the gunman kept firing, kept chipping away at it until the entire floor was littered with the sharp glass.

"Why didn't the breaking window trigger the security alarm?" she asked.

"Probably because this one wasn't wired into the system." It couldn't be lifted, which meant it wouldn't normally be a point of entry for someone trying to get in. It still wasn't, not with those jagged shards of glass sticking out all over.

"We'll just stay put," Theo said when the shots moved from the window to the wall. The wall adjacent to the shower. "The bullets can't get through the stones."

He hoped.

But the shots sure as heck could cause debris to fly through the air. It seemed as if the guy was trying to rip his way through the wall.

Theo's phone dinged, and he saw Gabriel's text message pop up on the screen. Are you both okay?

Fine, for now, Theo texted back.

He caught on to Ivy and lowered her until they were lying on the shower floor. It was larger than average size, but there still wasn't a lot of room with both of them in it. They were practically wrapped around each other.

I have a deputy and one of the hands moving in on the shooter, Gabriel added in his text a moment later. I think we can get this snake.

Theo was about to answer, but then he heard a strange sound. Definitely not an ordinary bullet this time. It was something else. Something that was about to make their situation a whole lot more dangerous than it already was.

A small metal canister.

It dropped onto the floor and started spewing tear gas.

Theo tucked the laptop under his arm, yanked Ivy to her feet and they started running. But it was already too late. The tear gas was burning their eyes and causing them to cough. Slowing them down, too. Not good. Because the gunman started firing bullets again, and this time Ivy and he were right in the path.

He crouched as low as he could, making sure Ivy did the same, and Theo somehow made his way to the door. The moment he had it unlocked and opened, he scrambled out in the hall, shutting the door behind them so it would hopefully contain some of the tear gas. Not all of it, though. It was already starting to seep right out at them.

Ivy was coughing so hard that she couldn't catch her breath, and he was certain her eyes felt as if they were on fire. His did, too, but Theo kept moving. Not downstairs, though. He took her to the hall bathroom. It had a tile floor but didn't have the stone protection of the other room. Plus, it had a massive window over the vanity.

It wouldn't take a gunman long at all to shoot through that.

But the last time Theo had checked, the ranch hand, Al, had been on that side of the house. Maybe he'd be able to put a stop to anyone who tried to put bullets or more tear gas into the room.

"Text Gabriel and make sure he's okay," Theo said, handing Ivy his phone. "I'll look on the laptop and see if we have any security cameras left."

They did. Three that were on the opposite side of the house from the shooter. Nothing much seemed to be happening there, but Theo heard more gunfire. This time, though, it came not from just one weapon but two. The gunman and someone else outside the house. Maybe a hand who had finally gotten in position to take out the shooter. Or at least stop him from sending more tear gas their way.

"Gabriel didn't answer," Ivy relayed to him. There was a new round of fear in her voice.

Theo was about to reassure her that Gabriel was probably just keeping watch and that nothing bad had happened to him. But he heard something that made Theo realize that might not be true.

The security alarm went off, the sound immediately blaring. And that wasn't the only sound. He also heard Gabriel's voice.

"Someone's in the house," Gabriel shouted.

Chapter Fifteen

Ivy hadn't thought her heart could beat any faster, but she'd been wrong about that. Just hearing what her brother said caused every part of her to start racing.

Her first instinct was to run downstairs and help Gabriel, but Theo kept his hand on her arm, no doubt to stop her from doing just that. Because it would have been a dangerous thing to do. She could get shot from friendly fire or cause such a distraction that it could get Gabriel killed. Still, it was almost impossible to just sit there and wait when the adrenaline was urging her to fight.

The security alarm went silent. Probably something Gabriel had done so he could hear what was going on. It was entirely possible that her brother had no idea where the intruder was in the house. Neither did she, but she took the laptop from Theo to try to have a look. There weren't any cameras inside the house, but maybe she could spot how the snake got inside.

Theo let go of her and opened the bathroom door a fraction so he could look out. He aimed his gun in the direction of the stairs, but if the intruder made it to that point, it meant he or she had gotten past Gabriel and the others. Rather than think about what that could mean, Ivy forced herself to focus on the computer screen.

And what she didn't see told her loads.

"No open windows or doors on the side, front or back of the house where we still have cameras," she relayed to him in a whisper.

That meant he'd come from the area between the two houses. Since the gunman was no longer shooting tear gas or bullets at them, it was entirely possible that he was in the process of trying to join his intruder comrade for a joint attack.

But how had the intruder gotten past the hands?

If it was just the one in the house, then it would make more sense. One person would have an easier time slipping into the house, especially on the side where they no longer had surveillance.

Ivy tried to pick through the darkness and see if there was anybody else out there. Al was no longer by the shed, and it took her a moment to find him. He was next to some shrubs that were only about ten yards from the back porch. He turned suddenly, taking aim at something on the blind spot side of the house, and he fired. Maybe he'd managed to take out anyone who was trying to sneak in.

Theo glanced back at the screen and muttered some profanity. At first she thought he'd done that because Al had likely killed someone who could have given them answers about all of this.

But no.

Ivy soon smelled more tear gas. And it didn't seem as if this was coming from the guest bath where they'd been but rather from the direction of the stairs.

"We'll have to get out," he told her.

No way could she argue with that, because Ivy was already starting to cough. It wouldn't be long before they would be so overtaken by the gas that they wouldn't be able to escape.

She wanted to ask him if that meant Gabriel had gotten out, but she soon saw that he had. On the computer screen, she saw Gabriel running from the front porch to the side of the shed where Al had been earlier.

Even though her brother was firing glances all around him, he was also doing something on his phone. A moment later Theo's own phone dinged, and she saw Gabriel's text.

There's a collapsible fire escape ladder on the shelf in my bedroom. Use it to get out the window.

She showed Theo the screen, and he immediately got her to her feet. He took his phone from her and shoved it back into his pocket.

Since he didn't know the location of Gabriel's room, Ivy pointed to the end of the hall. There was a window on the "safe" side of the house where Gabriel was, and they could get out that way.

First, though, they had to make it down a very long hall.

Theo positioned her ahead of him no doubt so he could try to shield her from any attacker who made it up the stairs. If someone was indeed on their way to try to kill them, then he or she had to be wearing a mask since there was now a tear gas mist blanketing not only the stairs but the hall, as well.

Ivy coughed the entire way to Gabriel's room, but with each step also came the fear. At any point someone could come up those stairs and start shooting. If that happened, Theo would be right in the line of fire.

She thought of Nathan and prayed nothing like this was going on at the new safe house. Maybe, just maybe, they could put an end to this tonight. Of course, that meant catching one of their attackers, and right now, that didn't seem probable.

The moment Ivy reached Gabriel's bedroom, she hurried inside. Theo rushed in behind her, closed the door and locked it. Ivy didn't waste even a second. While Theo stood guard, she went to the closet, but since she didn't know exactly where the portable metal ladder was, she had to waste precious time looking for it. She finally found it, folded up like an accordion, and ran to the window with it. Theo helped her with it.

Or at least that's what he started to do.

Before the shot blasted through the bedroom door.

The sound was deafening, and it felt as if it had blasted into her. Despite her shaking hands, Ivy forced herself to stay as steady as possible. Panicking now wouldn't do them any good. Instead, she hooked the ladder frame over the windowsill and let the chain rungs drop.

She spotted Gabriel and hoped he would be able to stop anyone from shooting them while they escaped, but even if he couldn't, Theo and she couldn't stay put. Especially not when another shot came at them. This one smacked into the wall right next to her.

"Go now!" Theo ordered her. "Leave the laptop so your hands will be free in case you have to shoot." And he returned fire.

Even though there was no way Theo could see the shooter, he obviously had a general idea of where the guy was because of the angle of the shots coming through the door.

Ivy scrambled out the window, and moving as fast as she could, she backed down the steps. Above her, Theo stayed put, volleying glances between the door, her and the yard. When she was halfway down, Theo followed her, and Ivy knew this was probably the best time for their attacker to go to the window and shoot at them.

If that happened, she prayed Gabriel would be able to stop him.

There were more shots from inside the house, and then they stopped. Did that mean the shooter was hurrying outside after them? Maybe. Ivy hadn't needed any other motivation to speed up their escape, but that reminder did it. When she got to the ground, she helped Theo and then turned so they could run to the shed.

But the sound of Theo's shout stopped her. "Gabriel, look out!"

Ivy saw it then. Something she definitely didn't want to see. A ski-masked gunman was behind Gabriel and was taking aim at him.

THEO IMMEDIATELY PULLED Ivy to the ground, though there wasn't much cover here by the side of the house. The only thing was a line of shrubs, but since bullets could easily go through those, he knew they couldn't stay there for long. Right now, though, there was a more immediate problem.

Gabriel.

Ivy's brother had to dive to the ground, too. In his case it was on the side of the shed facing them. And it was barely in time. Because the masked gunman fired a shot at him, and if Gabriel had stayed put, he would have taken that bullet.

Theo levered himself up and fired the gun, sending the man scrambling out of the line of fire. He didn't want to keep firing in the guy's direction, though, because he didn't know if there was a ranch hand out there.

"There's Al," Ivy whispered. Of course, she was trembling. Terrified, too. And Theo was scared for her.

Theo followed the direction of where she'd tipped her head, and he saw Al halfway between the shed and the barn. The very barn where there was a cruiser. Somehow, Theo needed to get Ivy there since it would be the safest place for her right now. Gabriel and he were obviously on the same page about that, and the text Theo got from him proved it.

I'll keep this thug occupied while you take Ivy to the barn, Gabriel said. It was a group message, and he'd included Al and several of the other hands and deputies.

Good. That way, all the people on their side knew where Ivy and he would be so they were less likely to get hit by friendly fire. Of course, it was the unfriendly fire that they had to worry about.

Gabriel and Al did, too.

Both Al and Gabriel adjusted their positions and got their weapons ready to fire. Theo didn't move yet. He waited for Gabriel to go to the other end of the shed, and he started firing in the direction of where they'd seen the gunman disappear. Al joined him in the shots, and that was Theo's signal to get Ivy out of there.

Theo pulled her to her feet, and while keeping low, they started running. It wasn't that far to the barn, but he knew that each step could be their last. In hindsight, this had been too dangerous of a plan. However, there was no turning back now.

They ran to the end of the house, and Theo paused only long enough to glance around the back to make sure someone wasn't lurking there. If someone was, maybe Al would be able to take them out. Just in case, though, Theo angled his gun as best he could, and then he caught on to Ivy's arm with his left hand. They made it to the barn door, and he pushed it open.

"Stay behind me," he warned Ivy.

Despite the gunfire that was going on in the yard, Theo still took a moment to look around the barn. The overhead light was off, but there was a light on in the tack room, and it gave him some decent visibility. He didn't see a gunman inside, but then, there were plenty of places to hide.

Including the cruiser.

It was impossible to watch every corner of the barn, so Theo turned Ivy so they were back-to-back. Not ideal, since she could end up facing a would-be killer head-on, but at this point nothing was ideal.

"Shoot at anything that moves," Theo told her, because there shouldn't be any hands or deputies in the barn.

Without taking his attention off their surroundings, he reached out and slid the barn door shut. Having the place closed off didn't help with the visibility because it shut out what little moonlight there was, but Theo didn't want to risk one of those stray shots coming in the opening.

"See anyone?" she asked.

He didn't. But that didn't mean someone wasn't there. "No," he answered. "Let's move closer to the cruiser."

Outside, the gunfire stopped, but that didn't give Theo any peace of mind. He hoped it didn't mean Gabriel or Al hadn't been shot. But it could also mean the gunmen were running away. While part of him would have liked that, he didn't especially want to give them a chance to regroup and come at them again.

"I don't see anyone in the cruiser," Ivy said.

Theo hadn't thought it possible, but her voice was trembling even more than it had before.

He, too, looked on the seat of the cruiser. No one. Well, unless someone was hiding on the floor. Someone could be on the other side of the vehicle, as well. That didn't help with the bad feeling that was snaking its way down his spine.

"When I open the cruiser door, get in," he instructed. "And slide across the seat so I can drive."

She moved to his side and gave a nod that was as shaky as the rest of her. She also still had a hard grip on her gun. A gun he wanted her to use if there was anyone lurking in the cruiser that they'd missed.

Theo shifted his body a little, and the moment he opened the door, Ivy scooted across the seat. She also locked the door on that side and then looked on the floor of the back seat.

"No one," she told him.

Theo was right behind her, and he locked up as well when he was behind the wheel. Thankfully, the keys were in the ignition, but he didn't start the engine. Not yet, anyway. He didn't want to risk the carbon monoxide building up while he was trying to contact Gabriel.

Plus, the sound of the engine might cover up someone trying to sneak up on them.

"Keep watch," Theo reminded her, though he was certain it wasn't a reminder she needed. Still, he wanted to be sure because texting Gabriel would divide his attention for a couple of seconds.

We're in the cruiser, he texted Ivy's brother. And Theo waited for a response.

A response didn't come, though, and after a couple of minutes crawled by, he had to consider that Gabriel might not be in a position to respond. He figured that Ivy realized that as well because her breathing kicked up a notch.

The silence came and everything suddenly seemed so still. As if waiting for something to happen. And something happened all right.

More gunshots came.

All of them slamming into the sides of the barn. Both of them. Theo didn't know exactly where the shooters were, but it felt as if they were closing in on them. He couldn't wait any longer for Gabriel's response. He needed to get Ivy out of there in case these thugs had something more than bullets to launch at them. They could have explosives.

"Hold on," he warned her.

The moment that Theo started the engine,

he hit the accelerator, and the cruiser crashed through the barn doors. But almost immediately he had to slam on the brakes. Because there in front of them were two gunmen.

And they had taken a hostage.

Chapter Sixteen

Because she wasn't wearing a seat belt, Ivy jolted forward when Theo brought the cruiser to a quick stop only a few yards in front of the back porch. And she didn't have to figure out why he'd done that.

There were two gunmen on the porch, their backs to the house.

They were both wearing ski masks, and they had their weapons pointed at Al's head. Al was standing in front of the two men, their human shield. They'd no doubt taken up that stance so that Theo or someone else couldn't shoot them.

Ivy's breath froze. Not her thoughts, though. The thoughts and fears came at her with a vengeance. These men were killers. Or that was their plan, anyway, and now the pair had them exactly where they wanted.

She pressed her left hand to her heart to try to steady it. Also tried to rein in her too-fast breathing. If she panicked now, it certainly wouldn't help them. No. She needed to keep a clear head and try to figure out how they could all get out of this alive.

But how?

They couldn't shoot at the men, and if they sped off, then they'd kill Al. At least Theo and she were in a bullet-resistant car, but that wouldn't help anyone else out there—especially Al. Ivy didn't know the hand that well, but he was out here because he'd been trying to protect her. That reminder twisted away at her, and once again she had to remind herself to stay calm.

"Step out of the cruiscr," one of the gunmen shouted.

"Stay put," Theo told her, and he didn't hesitate, either. However, he did lower his window a fraction so he could yell back an answer to the men. "Put down your weapons. There's no way you can get out of this alive."

If Theo's threat bothered them in the least, they didn't react to it. They certainly didn't put down their guns. Ivy had to wonder if these men had been in similar situations as Morris. Had their loved ones been taken as well to get them to do this or were they merely hired guns?

Either way, this situation could be deadly.

"Get out of the cruiser," the thug repeated. "If not, we start puttin' bullets in your friend here."

"Hell," Theo said under his breath, and he glanced around, probably looking for Gabriel or the other hands.

Ivy looked for them, too, and she spotted Gabriel still near the shed. He was at the wrong angle to have a shot to stop this, and if he stepped out from cover, one of the gunmen could easily shoot him.

Maybe someone could come through the front of the house to get to the men. But then she had to mentally shake her head. The house was probably still filled with tear gas.

"Who hired you?" Theo called out to the men. "Because whatever he or she is paying you, it's not enough for you to lose your lives. That's exactly what will happen, too, if you don't stop this now."

Even though she couldn't see their faces, Ivy thought the one who'd been doing all the talking laughed. "Just get out of the cruiser. I don't think you want your woman to watch as we shoot this guy."

No, Ivy didn't want to watch that, but she figured the moment Theo and she stepped out, these thugs would gun them down. She didn't want to see that, either, but they didn't have a lot of options here.

"Who exactly is it you're after?" Theo asked. "Me or Ivy?"

The two didn't jump to answer but did have a short whispered conversation. "Ivy. If she wants to save you or anybody else, then all she has to do is open the door and come to us."

"You're not going out there," Theo told her right off. "They won't want any of us alive because we're witnesses."

Because her mind was whirling with fear, she hadn't actually realized that. But it was true. Heck, the thugs probably had orders to kill them all.

But why?

That was the million-dollar question. And they still didn't have the answer. Because any of their suspects could have hired or coerced these men into doing this. It was even possible that their boss was nearby, waiting to make sure his or her orders had been carried out.

"I have men all around here," Gabriel called out.

Her brother had moved his position just a

little but was still thankfully behind cover. Or at least he was unless someone came from the back pasture. Hopefully, though, there were still hands out there to make sure that didn't happen.

"So do we," the thug answered back. "And time's up." He lowered his gun to Al's arm. "Either she gets out of the cruiser, or I fire the first shot. Just how much blood do you think he can lose before he dies?"

It was impossible for her not to think of Belinda Travers. She'd been shot and certainly hadn't survived. The same could happen to Al.

"I can't just sit here and watch him die," Ivy said.

Theo cursed again, glanced around as if trying to figure out what to do. "Get lower on the seat," he instructed. The moment she did that, he added to the men, "Give us just a few seconds. Ivy was hurt when we ran into the barn, and I'm trying to stop the bleeding. She's not in any shape to stand right now."

Ivy doubted the men would buy the lie, but it seemed to give them a little time because the thugs had another whispered conversation.

"They're wearing masks," Theo said, but it sounded as if he was talking to himself more than her. "The man who attacked Morris's family didn't wear one."

She considered that for a moment. "You think these are men you know?"

"Maybe." Theo shook his head. "Or maybe they're just cocky enough to think they can kill us all and escape." He turned back to the window. "Ivy needs an ambulance," he shouted to the men.

Theo then took out his phone, and while keeping watch of the situation on the porch, he also sent a text to someone. Probably Gabriel. Because a few seconds later, Ivy saw her brother glance down at his phone screen.

"Put on your seat belt," Theo told her.

Ivy was certain her eyes widened. "Why? What are you going to do?"

"Play a game of chicken to get these guys to scatter so that Gabriel can pick them off. But I want you belted in and as far down on the seat as you can go in case something goes wrong."

And there was plenty that could go wrong.

She managed a nod and did as he said. Ivy also kept her gun ready just in case this situation went from bad to worse.

"Hold on," Theo said the moment they were in place, and he hit the accelerator.

The cruiser lurched forward, but Ivy

couldn't see what was going on. However, she could hear it. The men cursed.

And then a shot blasted into the windshield.

THEO HAD ALREADY braced himself for the shot that came right at them. The ones that followed, too. He gave the steering wheel a sharp turn so that his side of the cruiser bashed into the back porch railing. The impact certainly jarred Ivy and him. Seemed to jar the house, too.

But it didn't stop the gunmen.

Four more bullets came crashing into the cruiser's engine and his window, cracking and webbing the glass to the point that it was nearly impossible for him to see.

He could hear, though.

And what he heard was Gabriel returning fire. Good. It was just as Theo had instructed him to do with that text he'd sent him.

Judging from the angle of the returned fire, Gabriel did indeed have the right angle or at least enough of one to get those gunmen. Maybe that meant Al had scrambled out of the way so they could put a quick end to this.

Since the side of the cruiser was now directly in front of the porch, Theo tried to peer through what was left of the glass. It took him a few seconds, but he saw the gunmen. Both were now in the back doorway of the house and didn't seem to be reacting to the tear gas. Maybe they had some kind of filtering equipment beneath those ski masks.

Both of the gunmen were leaning out from cover to continue firing. The one on the left was shooting into the cruiser. The one on the right was aiming in Gabriel's direction. No doubt to try to pin him down.

There was no sign of Al.

It was possible the thugs had dragged him into the house, and because the lights were off, Theo couldn't see anything in there, much less try to figure out if the man was alive. Later, he would need to do that, but for now he had a much more immediate problem.

There was another round of shots, these going into the engine, and it didn't take long for it to start spewing steam. They'd obviously shot out the radiator, which would make it impossible for Theo to use it for an escape. They certainly wouldn't get far enough away from those gunmen to do any good. Still, he'd known that right from the start. That meant they had to make their stand here and hope Gabriel and the hand could do enough to capture the shooters.

Now that they'd disabled the engine, the shooter shifted back to his window. The bullets tore a big enough hole in the glass that the shots started coming into the interior of the cruiser. He was betting these guys had a lot of ammo, and as long as the one kept Gabriel out of the picture, it meant the other one could continue blasting until he shot Ivy and him.

Another chunk of the glass came flying right at him, and Theo had no choice but to duck down. He didn't stay there, though. He came up off the seat, and he used one of the holes in the window to take aim so he could fire. He double tapped the trigger and sent the thugs ducking back inside.

It didn't last.

After only a few seconds, the thugs started shooting again. This time the glass fell right onto Ivy. She quickly lifted her hand, putting it over the back of her head, but Theo knew that wouldn't be enough to keep her protected.

The shots continued, coming at them nonstop, but there was other gunfire, too. It was coming from the pasture behind the barn. Probably one or more of the hands. Hopefully, that meant they knew that Al was out of the way so that he wouldn't be hit.

"Stay put," Theo told Ivy.

As expected, she lifted her head just enough to make eye contact with him, and he saw her shake her head. "You're not going out there."

It darn sure wasn't something he wanted to do. Not with bullets seemingly coming from every direction, but he couldn't just sit there and let Ivy be hit. Something that could happen any moment now that the shots were coming into the vehicle.

"I'll use the door for cover," he told her.

She still shook her head and reached for him. Theo wanted to take the time to reassure her, but maybe that wasn't even possible, anyway. He put his hand on the door handle.

And then heard the sound crack through the air.

Not another bullet. It was a tear gas canister, and it smacked onto the ground just a few feet from the cruiser.

Hell.

Theo ditched his idea to open the door and instead try to start the engine to get them out of there. No such luck, though. The gunmen had seen to that. This had likely been their intention all along, and Theo had no choice but to move Ivy.

"We'll go out your side," he told her. "Open the door and get out but stay low. Wait for me, and then we'll run to the shed where Gabriel is."

It wasn't an especially good plan, but he didn't have a lot of options here. Especially not with the tear gas starting to ooze its way into the cruiser. His only hope was that the tear gas would hide his and Ivy's escape. Then he had to hope they didn't collapse along the way. It wouldn't be a long run, but it would feel like a marathon with that gas burning their eyes and lungs.

Coughing again, Ivy threw open the door, and she practically tumbled out, landing in a crouching position on the ground. Theo kept low since the bullets were still coming, and he crawled toward her.

"Watch out!" Gabriel shouted.

Despite the gunfire, Theo heard him loud and clear, but he had no idea why Gabriel had yelled out that warning. Not until he saw the movement.

Someone was walking out of that cloud of tear gas.

That someone had a gun, and he latched onto Ivy, knocking away her gun. In the same motion, he took aim.

And the man fired.

THE SHOT WAS so close to Ivy that the sound blasted through her head. She braced herself to feel the pain from being hit. But nothing.

Well, nothing other than the pain in her ears from the noise.

From what she could tell, the shot had gone into the ground right next to her. Maybe he'd just missed. Or else it could have been some kind of warning shot. If so, it had certainly gotten her attention.

Despite the man's having hold of her and that fired shot, she was alive, and she needed to do something to keep it that way. Ivy turned, ready to push her attacker away before he could fire again, but she was already too late. He hooked his arm around her and put the gun to her head. Worse, he was in position so neither Theo nor her brother might have a clean shot to take out this guy.

She tried to elbow the man in his gut, but he only tightened his grip on her until he had her in a choke hold. It was already hard enough to breathe because of the tear gas, and that certainly didn't help.

The man, however, probably had no trouble breathing. That's because he was wearing a gas mask. Ivy caught a glimpse of it when she managed to glance back at him.

"Let her go," Theo growled. That's when Ivy realized he had taken up cover behind the back of the cruiser.

Of course, the man didn't release her, and he didn't respond to Theo's demand. He just started dragging her onto the porch. Only a few steps, and he would have her inside where there were at least two other gunmen waiting.

She forced herself to stay as calm as she could. Which probably wasn't very calm. But she needed to think. Needed to do something to make sure no one got killed before she even tried to diffuse this.

"If this is about my husband's money," she said. "We can work this out."

Again, no response. So if Lacey was indeed behind this, then she'd convinced the men not to bargain with her. Maybe by kidnapping their families. Maybe because Lacey had just paid them too well.

The man just kept dragging her, and the moment they reached the doorway, he pulled her inside. Ivy had been right about the gunmen being there. One was on each side of the door. A door they didn't close. They stayed there, no doubt ready to shoot anyone who came after her.

At least the tear gas inside had thinned out enough for her to breathe. But the bad news was that the goon still had her in a choke hold.

"I gave birth to Travis's only grandchild," she tried again. She needed to hit some kind of nerve so she knew who she was dealing with. "He wouldn't like it if anything bad happened to me."

The man still didn't say anything. That didn't mean August wasn't behind this, though. In fact, it didn't rule out anyone.

"Everything's in place," one of the thugs said to her captor.

She didn't recognize the voice, but it made her wonder if Theo would. Ivy peered out through the door but could no longer see him. Could no longer see Gabriel, either, but maybe either he or one of the hands was making his way to the front of the house where the man was taking her.

The lights were all off in the house, but Ivy looked around for anything she could try to grab so she could club the guy. The only thing she could spot was a vase on a table in the family room, but when she reached for it, the man snapped her back so hard that Ivy nearly blacked out from the pain and loss of breath. She couldn't try that again, not while he had her in a choke hold, anyway, or he might kill her. Still, she didn't intend to go with him without a fight.

But where was he taking her?

Better yet, how did he plan on getting her off the ranch?

She soon had the answer to her last question. There was a third masked thug by the front door, and he opened it. When the man dragged her onto the front porch, she saw the black SUV parked by the steps. Maybe this was the vehicle the shooter in the old house had used. It could have been driven up the path between the two houses. Given the limited visibility from the gas fog and the darkness, it would have been hard to see. Still, she couldn't imagine one of the hands not spotting it. Did that mean these thugs had killed them?

It sickened Ivy to think that could have happened, but with all the gunfire going on, it was impossible to know.

There was a new round of shots. This time at the back of the house where she'd last seen Al and those two hired thugs. Gabriel was in that general area, too, and she prayed that none of them had been hit.

In one last-ditch effort to save herself, Ivy dropped down her weight, trying to throw the man off balance, but he just hooked his other arm around her waist and kept going. Straight for that SUV.

"Wesley?" someone called out.

Theo.

Ivy couldn't see him, but judging from the sound of his voice, he was on the side of the house toward the front of the SUV.

As the man had done the other times Theo or she had spoken to him, he didn't say a word, but she felt his arm tense just enough to let her know that Theo had been right. This was Wesley or else someone working for him.

But why would Wesley want her?

"Ivy has nothing to do with this," Theo continued. "This is between you and me."

Again, her captor's arm tensed, but he still didn't talk.

"You don't want me to hear your voice," Theo added. "But I recognized one of your hired guns. He's a criminal informant. I know because I've used him myself. My guess is you got him to do this for cheap or else you threatened him with arrest. Either way, it doesn't matter. This ends here."

The gunmen at the front door came onto the

porch, took aim at Theo and fired. Ivy's heart went to her throat, and her breath stalled in her chest until she realized Theo had dropped back in the nick of time. He hadn't been hit.

However, he could be.

In fact, this could end badly for all of them. That's why she had to try to bargain with this man.

"I'll go with you," she told him, "but you need to leave Theo and everyone else here alone."

Wesley or whoever this was certainly didn't jump to agree to that. The man started backing her down the front porch steps, and it would be only a matter of a few seconds before he had her in that SUV. Heaven knew then where he'd take her. Or what he'd do to her. Plus, that would leave the hired guns in place to keep attacking Gabriel, Theo and the hands.

Theo came out from cover again, and he fired at the gunman who wasn't holding Ivy. The bullet hit the thug and despite the fact that he was wearing a Kevlar vest, he dropped onto the porch. That's when Ivy saw the blood and realized Theo's shot had gone into his neck. If he wasn't dead already, he soon would be.

Her captor mumbled some profanity under

his breath and started moving her even faster. It was a mistake. Because it gave Ivy the chance to trip on the last step. She paid for it with pain when he bashed her upside her head with his gun, but that only got him out of position to shoot Theo.

Theo, however, was in position.

Now that Theo had a clean shot, he didn't hesitate; he fired three shots. All three bullets slammed into the guy's chest. He was also wearing Kevlar, but the bullets must have knocked the wind out of him because he fell, his head smacking onto the side of the SUV.

The driver's-side door flew open, and the gunman inside took aim at Theo. However, he barely had brought up his hand when someone fired. Not the gunman or Theo. It was Gabriel. He was now in the doorway of the house, and he'd taken out the thug with a shot to the head.

While Theo ran toward her, Ivy kicked the gun out of the fallen man's hand, and it landed a few feet away. Once Theo reached her, he maneuvered her next to the porch railing, where she'd have a little cover in case there was another attack, and he went to the man. The guy was wheezing and clutching his chest, but Theo ripped off the gas mask.

It was Wesley all right.

He cursed Theo and then smiled, his head dropping back onto the ground.

"You just signed their death warrants," Wesley said.

Theo was no doubt about to ask Wesley what he meant by that, but then she heard something she didn't want to hear.

An explosion.

She whipped toward the sound of the blast. Her parents' old house. And it was now in flames.

Chapter Seventeen

Theo cursed. He hadn't exactly relaxed, but he had thought the worst of the danger was over. Maybe not, though. His instincts were to go running to the old house, to make sure no one was inside, but that could be a trap. Something that Wesley had set up in case he failed here.

Which he had.

The agent was moaning in pain, but he still had that stupid smirk on his face. A smirk that could be there because he'd put someone in that house. Someone who was now dying because of the fire. The flames were quickly eating their way through the place, and even if they could get the fire department out right away, it might still be too late to save it.

"Three of the ranch hands are on the way down there," Gabriel said after reading a text. "And Edwin's just up the road. He'll be arriving at the old house in just a couple of minutes."

Maybe that would be enough, because it was also possible that Wesley had stashed the rest of his hired guns near there. Hired guns who would kill anyone who came their way.

Theo checked the SUV to make sure no one else was inside. It was empty. Theo also picked up Wesley's gun and shoved it in the back waistband of his jeans.

"Where are the gunmen who were at the back of the house?" Theo asked Gabriel.

"Dead," Gabriel answered while he tossed Theo a pair of plastic cuffs that he took from his pocket. "Al's back there, and he's keeping watch to make sure no one else sneaks up on us. The hands in the pastures are reporting that they're not seeing any other gunmen. Not live ones, anyway. They had to shoot a couple of them. Jace has rounded up a couple of them, too."

Theo released the breath he hadn't even noticed he was holding. Of course, there could still be a straggler out there, but maybe that person would just surrender now that his boss had been captured.

From the end of the trail, Theo saw the cruiser lights as the vehicle pulled to a stop near the burning house. Edwin, no doubt. At least now the hands had law enforcement help.

Gabriel made a call to someone else, but Theo didn't wait to hear who he was talking to. He first cuffed Wesley, and since it was still too dangerous for Ivy to be outside in the open where a sniper could pick her off, he put her on the passenger's seat of the SUV.

"Stay down," Theo warned her.

She gave a shaky nod and caught on to his arm when he started to move away. That's when he spotted the marks on her throat. Bruises and scrapes from Wesley putting her in that choke hold. It sickened him to think of just how close she'd come to dying.

And all because of him.

"I'm so sorry," Theo said.

Ivy shook her head, took hold of the front of his shirt and pulled him to her. She kissed him. It didn't last long. Just enough to soothe some of the raw nerves inside him. Still, he wanted to beat Wesley senseless for doing this.

Standing guard in front of Ivy, Theo turned so he could face Wesley. "Who's in the old house?"

"Just tying up some loose ends." The smirk finally faded, and he glared up at Theo. "You might as well go ahead and kill me. You know what they do to former agents in prison?"

Yeah, he did, but since this piece of slime had tried to kill Ivy, Theo didn't care what happened to the man.

"Who are the loose ends?" Theo pressed.

Wesley groaned in pain. Probably because he had cracked ribs. Or maybe the realization of what he'd done was finally hitting him. "One loose end," he amended. "Someone who helped me fund this little operation. Don't worry. I sent proof of the money trail to the sheriff's office so you'll know who paid for all these hired guns."

Hell. That could maybe be August or Lacey. Theo was hoping, though, that it was just a bluff and the only person dead in that house was the guy who'd fired those rounds of tear gas.

"It wasn't supposed to work this way," Wesley mumbled.

"No. If things had gone according to your plan, you would have kidnapped Ivy and used her to get me to do whatever you wanted me to do."

That could involve anything from destroying evidence to murder. Because Wesley knew that Theo would do anything to get Ivy back.

But there was another angle to this.

If Lacey had been the one to "fund" all of this, then maybe Ivy had been as much of a target as Theo. This attack could have been designed to kill them both.

"The fire department, an ambulance and two more backup cruisers are on the way," Gabriel relayed after yet another call. "I'll stay here with Ivy and you until we're sure it's safe."

Good. But judging from Gabriel's tone and the way his gaze kept darting to the burning house, that's where he wanted to be. So did Theo, but it was too big of a risk to leave Ivy alone. Once backup arrived, Theo could get her out of there. Maybe they'd have more answers by then. Answers that Wesley could give them.

"I had no proof you did anything wrong in that botched raid," Theo told the man.

"Didn't matter. You suspected I had something to do with it, and you wouldn't have let go of it."

Theo shook his head. "I didn't suspect it until the attacks started."

Wesley made a sound as if he didn't believe that. And maybe he was right. In the back of Theo's mind, he'd always felt something was wrong. He wouldn't have let go of it, either, and eventually he would have started digging. That digging would have led him to Wesley.

"Did you think you could kill and silence everyone who could figure out you were dirty?" Ivy asked Wesley.

Wesley turned his head to the side, spared her a glance before making a weary sigh. "Yes. You don't understand. I can't go to jail." He groaned. "I'll die there."

"You didn't mind killing innocent people to save yourself. That makes you a coward," Theo told him. "And Belinda's kidnapping and murder is going to put you on death row."

Gabriel's phone buzzed, and he answered it right away but again didn't put it on speaker. Nor did he say anything. For several slow, crawling moments, Gabriel just listened to whatever the caller was telling him.

"The ambulance should be here any minute," Gabriel finally said, and he ended the call. He looked at Theo. "It's Lacey."

"She came here with Wesley?" Ivy asked her brother.

"Was forced here, according to what she said. She's alive, but Wesley had stun-gunned her and left her in the house with a firebomb that was on a timer before he and the thug came over here. She wasn't burned but took in a lot of smoke before the hands pulled her out."

Now it was Ivy's turn to curse. "Lacey is the one who funded Wesley."

Gabriel nodded. "Wesley apparently went to her with the plan, but she's saying she didn't have anything to do with any deaths. When Wesley tied her up, though, he told her he was going to pin all of this on her by making it look as if she'd died while launching an attack."

Yeah, and it might have worked, too. If they hadn't gotten lucky.

"I had no idea she'd go this far," Ivy said. She tried, and failed, to choke back a hoarse sob. "Nathan could have been hurt, or worse." Another sob. "We all could have been."

Theo kept watch, but he pulled Ivy into his arms for a short hug. It didn't help. Nothing would at this point. That's why he kissed her.

"I love you," he whispered. "And we're going to get through this."

She blinked, clearly surprised by his L-word bombshell. He'd never told her that, and she probably thought it was the adrenaline talking. It wasn't. He'd always loved Ivy. But now hadn't been the time to tell her.

And she certainly wasn't telling him she felt the same.

Definitely the wrong time, because Ivy had enough whirling through her head without adding that.

Theo got a good distraction—he heard the sirens. Lots of them. And he knew it wouldn't be long before he could finally get Ivy out of there. He took out his phone and handed it to her.

"Call Jameson," he instructed. "See if you can talk to Nathan."

The moment the cruiser pulled into the driveway, Gabriel came down the porch steps. "Arrest him," Gabriel told the two deputies who got out of the cruiser, and he tipped his head to Wesley.

Gabriel must have already instructed the ambulance where to go because it sped past them and went to his parents' house. The fire truck was right behind it. The two cruisers, however, came to Gabriel's. Both stopped, and a pair of deputies got out of the first vehicle and a third one exited the cruiser behind them.

Ivy kept watch of everything going on, but she continued her conversation on the phone. Obviously, she'd reached Jameson and could assure him that everything was okay. Well, as okay as it could be considering just how close she'd come to dying.

"Wesley said he sent something to the sheriff's office," Theo told one of the deputies who approached him. Her name was Susan Bowie, someone he'd known since he was a kid.

Susan nodded. "A courier delivered some papers about thirty minutes ago."

Right about the time the attack had started—though it certainly felt as if the gunfire had lasted a lot longer than that. "The papers implicated Lacey Vogel?"

Another nod. "They're records to show withdrawals from an offshore account in Ms. Vogel's name. There were other bank accounts to show where the money went."

Theo was betting they could match the deposits to the dead gunmen scattered over the ranch. Lacey had been an idiot to use a bank to pay for all of this, or else she'd been so hell-bent on revenge that she didn't take precautions. Of course, Wesley wouldn't have helped with those precautions, either, since he'd probably intended to set Lacey up right from the beginning. Lacey had helped him by making herself a prime suspect.

Gabriel stayed right by Wesley until Susan and a male deputy hauled the man into the cruiser. Theo watched, too, and even Ivy got one last look at Wesley before the deputy shut the door. At least Wesley wasn't smirking or smiling now. It had probably set in that he would never be in a position to hurt them again.

Nor Lacey, for that matter.

The ambulance would take her to the hospital, but after that, she'd be arrested. Not only had Wesley ratted out Lacey as funding this attack, Lacey herself had admitted to paying for the thugs used in the attacks.

"Susan, you and Mick go ahead and take Wesley to jail," Gabriel told the deputy. "Read him his rights. Do everything by the book." After Susan nodded, he turned to the third deputy. "I want you to stay here and help Edwin wrap things up. I need to use your cruiser to take my sister somewhere."

Gabriel didn't say where that somewhere was, but Theo figured it was the safe house. There was nothing that would get that look of terror off Ivy's face faster than seeing her son.

Their son, Theo mentally corrected.

He figured it would help settle him down, as well.

Theo hurried when he helped Ivy from the SUV and into the cruiser, and she ended her call with Jameson, probably so she could hear an update from Gabriel and him. As they'd done on their other trips, Theo got in the back seat with her, and as soon as Gabriel was behind the wheel, he took off.

"Please tell me we're going to the safe house," Ivy said.

"We are," Gabriel answered. "I'll drop you two off there and come back here and deal with the investigation."

That wouldn't be a fast or easy thing to do. Heaven knew how many dead bodies there were, and there was a huge crime scene to process. If there were any gunmen left alive, they would also have to be arrested and interrogated. Gabriel would be putting in a lot of long hours and all because of a dirty agent and a greedy stepdaughter.

"Wesley sent bank documents to the sheriff's office," Theo told Ivy and Gabriel, too, in case he hadn't heard what Susan had said earlier. "It should be what you need to bring murder charges against Lacey."

"Murder?" Ivy repeated on a rise of breath.

"Yeah. Because of Belinda, the CI and McKenzie. Since Lacey paid for the attacks, both Wesley and she will be charged."

Ivy stayed quiet a moment, probably letting

that sink in. Then fresh tears sprang to her eyes. "It's over." Her voice was mostly breath and filled with relief. So, the tears weren't from sadness this time.

"It's over," Theo assured her.

Gabriel took the turn from the ranch, and once he got onto the main road, he sped up. "The safe house isn't far. Ten minutes or so. That should give you two a little time to…talk or something."

Theo met Gabriel's gaze in the rearview mirror, and even though Gabriel didn't come out and say it, he seemed to be telling Theo to go for it. But what Gabriel didn't know was that Theo already had. He'd told Ivy he loved her, and she hadn't said a word about her feelings for him.

Maybe their pasts were just too painful for her to put behind her. Hell, maybe she didn't even want him in her and Nathan's lives. Well, tough. He was going to be there. At least in Nathan's, anyway.

"I'm taking that desk job in San Antonio," Theo said. Unlike Ivy's voice, there was no relief in his. But there was some anger. "I could try to put in for a transfer to Houston or wherever you end up—"

She slid her hand around the back of his

neck, pulled him to her and kissed him. Hard. That was probably the fastest way to get him to shut up.

"I love you," she said when she broke for air.

Ivy went back for another kiss. Apparently, that was another way to get him to hush, because it stunned him to silence. Strange considering how much he wanted to say to her. But at the moment, he just mentally repeated those words.

And savored them.

Until she'd said it, Theo hadn't realized just how much he'd wanted to hear them. Not just now. But for years. Because that's how long he'd been in love with Ivy.

"I want to stay at the ranch," she continued, her breath as ragged as his was. A good kiss could do that. "Maybe build a house." She paused. "With Nathan and you."

That felt like a punch. A good one. Because it caused a warmth to go through him from head to toe.

"You'd sure as hell better ask her to marry you," Gabriel grumbled. "After all, you did get her pregnant ten years ago. She's crazy in love with you, and Nathan needs a dad. Heck, Ivy needs *you*."

Theo hadn't been certain that Gabriel was listening, but obviously he was. And he was right. That wasn't just Ivy's big brother talking. This was right between Ivy and him, and the past was the past.

"Well?" Theo said, turning to her. "Will you marry me?"

Just in case she had any notion of saying no, Theo kissed her. He made sure it was long and deep. Made sure he poured his heart into it, too. Which wasn't hard to do. Because Ivy already had his heart.

"Yes," she managed to get out before the kissing continued.

Later, they could celebrate. And he could get her an engagement ring. Later, there'd be time for a lot of things—like living the rest of their lives together. But for now, it had to wait, because Gabriel took the turn to the safe house.

The moment they pulled into the driveway, the door opened, and Theo saw something that made this complete.

Nathan.

His boy was there, right between Jameson and Jodi. And Nathan was grinning from ear to ear.

"Mom," he called out to Ivy.

Ivy scrambled out of the car, and before she made it to Nathan, Theo saw more tears in her eyes. This time he knew for certain they were happy ones. She pulled Nathan into her arms, kissed him and kept on kissing him until the boy was laughing.

"Dad," Nathan said when Ivy finally let go of him. He went to Theo and hugged him.

Theo had to blink back some happy tears himself. Not very manly to cry, but he suddenly realized he had everything he'd ever wanted right here. He gathered both Ivy and Nathan in his arms and held on tight.

* * * * *

Get 2 Free Books,
Plus 2 Free Gifts—
just for trying the Reader Service!

YES! Please send me 2 FREE Harlequin Presents® novels and my 2 FREE gifts (gifts are worth about $10 retail). After receiving them, if I don't wish to receive any more books, I can return the shipping statement marked "cancel." If I don't cancel, I will receive 6 brand-new novels every month and be billed just $4.55 each for the regular-print edition or $5.55 each for the larger-print edition in the U.S., or $5.49 each for the regular-print edition or $5.99 each for the larger-print edition in Canada. That's a saving of at least 11% off the cover price! It's quite a bargain! Shipping and handling is just 50¢ per book in the U.S. and 75¢ per book in Canada*. I understand that accepting the 2 free books and gifts places me under no obligation to buy anything. I can always return a shipment and cancel at any time. The free books and gifts are mine to keep no matter what I decide.

Please check one: ☐ Harlequin Presents® Regular-Print   ☐ Harlequin Presents® Larger-Print
                              (106/306 HDN GMWK)   (176/376 HDN GMWK)

Name _____ (PLEASE PRINT) _____

Address _____ Apt. # _____

City _____ State/Prov. _____ Zip/Postal Code _____

Signature (if under 18, a parent or guardian must sign) _____

Mail to the Reader Service:

IN U.S.A.: P.O. Box 1341, Buffalo, NY 14240-8531
IN CANADA: P.O. Box 603, Fort Erie, Ontario L2A 5X3

Want to try two free books from another series?
Call 1-800-873-8635 or visit www.ReaderService.com.

* Terms and prices subject to change without notice. Prices do not include applicable taxes. Sales tax applicable in N.Y. Canadian residents will be charged applicable taxes. Offer not valid in Quebec. This offer is limited to one order per household. Books received may not be as shown. Not valid for current subscribers to Harlequin Presents books. All orders subject to approval. Credit or debit balances in a customer's account(s) may be offset by any other outstanding balance owed by or to the customer. Please allow 4 to 6 weeks for delivery. Offer available while quantities last.

Your Privacy—The Reader Service is committed to protecting your privacy. Our Privacy Policy is available online at www.ReaderService.com or upon request from the Reader Service.

We make a portion of our mailing list available to reputable third parties that offer products we believe may interest you. If you prefer that we not exchange your name with third parties, or if you wish to clarify or modify your communication preferences, please visit us at www.ReaderService.com/consumerchoice or write to us at Reader Service Preference Service, P.O. Box 9062, Buffalo, NY 14240-9062. Include your complete name and address.

HP17R3

Get 2 Free Books,

Plus 2 Free Gifts—

just for trying the
Reader Service!

HRLP17R3

Get 2 Free Books,
Plus 2 Free Gifts -
just for trying the *Reader Service!*

STRS17R2

READERSERVICE.COM

Manage your account online!

- Review your order history
- Manage your payments
- Update your address

*We've designed the
Reader Service website
just for you.*

Enjoy all the features!

- Discover new series available to you, and read excerpts from any series.
- Respond to mailings and special monthly offers.
- Browse the Bonus Bucks catalog and online-only exculsives.
- Share your feedback.

Visit us at:

ReaderService.com

RS16R